Whispers of Mermaids and Wonderful Things

Children's Poetry *and* Verse *from* Atlantic Canada

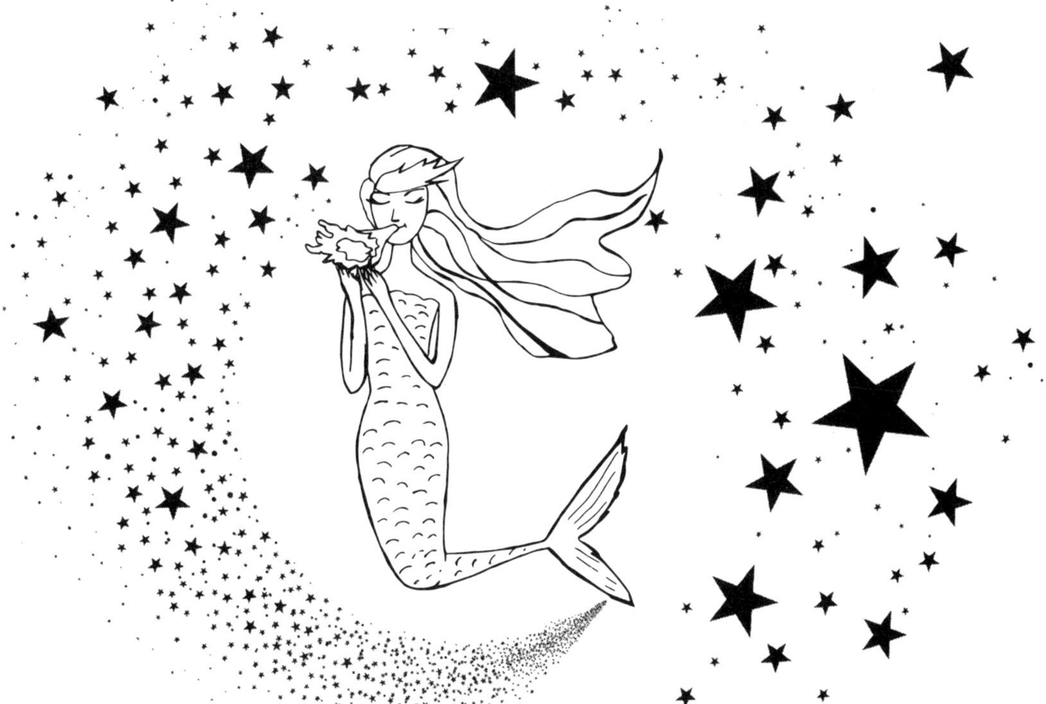

Edited by *Sheree Fitch* and *Anne Hunt*

Copyright © 2017, Nimbus Publishing

All rights reserved. No part of this book may be reproduced, stored in a retrieval system or transmitted in any form or by any means without the prior written permission from the publisher, or, in the case of photocopying or other reprographic copying, permission from Access Copyright, 1 Yonge Street, Suite 1900, Toronto, Ontario M5E 1E5.

Nimbus Publishing Limited
3731 Mackintosh St, Halifax, NS, B3K 5A5
(902) 455-4286 nimbus.ca

Printed and bound in Canada

NB1252

Cover illustration (centre): Lloyd Fitzgerald
Design: Heather Bryan

All reasonable efforts have been made by the publisher to contact, and receive permissions from, copyright holders to the poems included in this anthology. Any questions regarding copyright are to be directed to the publisher.

Library and Archives Canada Cataloguing in Publication

    Whispers of mermaids and wonderful things : Atlantic Canadian poetry and verse for children / edited by Sheree Fitch and Anne Hunt.

    ISBN 978-1-77108-471-0 (hardcover)

1. Children's poetry, Canadian (English)--Atlantic Provinces. 2. Children's poetry, Canadian (English)--21st century. I. Fitch, Sheree, editor II. Hunt, Anne, 1940-, editor

PS8295.5.A85W45 2017   jC811'.6080928209715   C2016-908007-2

Nimbus Publishing acknowledges the financial support for its publishing activities from the Government of Canada, the Canada Council for the Arts, and from the Province of Nova Scotia. We are pleased to work in partnership with the Province of Nova Scotia to develop and promote our creative industries for the benefit of all Nova Scotians.

Contents

Foreword by Dr. Russ Hunt ~ 1

The Story of this Book ~ 5

Poems & Verse

    Wordplay ~ 9

    Weather ~ 29

    Wonder ~ 51

    Whimsy ~ 79

    Warmth ~ 105

    Whispers ~ 127

Afterword by Dr. Sue Fisher ~ 143

Poet Biographies ~ 147

Permissions ~ 165

Index of Authors & Poems ~ 168

On the Road to Everywhere

On the road to everywhere
In the midst of the galaxy
I met a child
With eyes that smiled
Here's what she said to me:
"Yesterday, I saw the moon
But it wasn't in the sky—
It was in a book
It sounded round
The gold got in my eye.
You see
I learned to read—
YES!
Now I understand
Now I know it's possible
To hold
      the moon
           in my hands."

Sheree Fitch

Foreword

A toddler curls up in the warm place under a parent's arm, both focused on the open book in front of them. The parent's voice translates the silent mysterious symbols on the page into real language, language they attend to, understand, and respond to, together.

We all know this is an important scene, one of the miracles of human society. We don't, though, reflect very often or very deeply on why this is so. We say learning to read is important, and we often stop right there, letting the idea rest on the convenient assumption that it's about exchanging information, about learning the "skills" that will let a child grow into an adult who can "succeed in school" and "earn a living." In truth, though, that sort of mechanical process is by far the least important thing happening in front of that open book.

What makes us fully human is our ability to imagine the mental states and processes of the people around us. Psychologists call this, awkwardly, "theory of mind," which makes it seem pretty distant from our everyday experience. But in fact, it's exactly this empathy that lets us know what Mom means when she says, "Well, that hair is a bird's nest, isn't it?" It isn't, of course, only that she doesn't mean there's a bird somewhere nearby; it also means that we all share an image of what the nest a bird makes looks like, and know together that birds are nice, that nests are comfy, and at the same time that a bird's nest on your head isn't quite appropriate, and that you and Mom are sharing all that.

This leads to—no, is central to—the ability to understand the figures of speech that make language more than a telegraph system: metaphors, sarcasm, irony. The ability to understand the language that goes beyond literal information is central to our participation in the society around us. If that sounds exaggerated, consider what would be lost to our society if, after a delicious meal, someone next to you said, "Well, that was really horrible." Imagine you missed the irony and thought there was a disagreement about the meal, rather than sharing the presumption that it was so good any negative comment would be immediately recognized, by both speaker and listeners, as absurd.

We almost never notice the extent to which our language is drenched in, is composed of, figures of speech which depend on our already sharing values, assumptions, connections, with each other. And, most centrally, recognizing the sharing; knowing, without anyone saying it, that the speaker is expecting you to recognize her language as intending something, as being the utterance of someone whose mind is deeply like your own. Who knows that you know that she knows.

And where does the ability to use language that way come from? Consider that toddler, the parent, the book. Consider how the toddler, in order to understand what is happening at all, has to come to feel the relations between the voice of the mother, the voice of the author, and the marks on the page. As the mother and toddler share the surprise of the turned page, the bounce of the new and unexpected word or idea, the three become one experience, and the child's understanding of other human beings' experiences can be shared through that page.

And so, what about a book of poems? A book of poems coming from our shared social context, written without the academic assumption that to be "good," poetry needs to be nearly incomprehensible without the help of a scholar or critic or teacher? A book using language that can build on the assumption that we already share experience of a world, of how that world is connected together, and how people act in it, to extend and deepen our ability to use language to participate in that world together? So when Mom reads to you, or when you read yourself, something like Bill Bauer's amazing "Tantrum Poem III," you know, and learn, that everyone can share the complex amusement at the small child's refusing to eat something everyone else agrees is just fine, and imagining the absurd consequences.

Contemplate how wonderfully complicated that experience is. It's the voice of someone else, a stranger, someone named Bill Bauer, pretending to be a child, and it's Dad's voice—or perhaps now your own—taking the same language on, knowing that it's play, that there is no child with a wad of meat stuffed in a cheek, knowing that it's funny, and at the same time understanding just what it would be like to be that child, imagining how, thirty-five years from now with the meat still there, "everyone / Will say and won't I be glad when they do / What cruel parents he must have had / To drive him to do such a thing as that." The richness of that social experience—of that understanding, tolerant amusement—is deeply humanizing.

But what about a book of poems "from Atlantic Canada"? To engage with the voices far from us, the voices of the world, we begin with the voices near to us, the voices of Mom and Dad, the voices of family, the voices of neighbours. And the voices of our shared cultures and surroundings. The recognition of our own experiences can be shared, can be made into metaphors, can become opportunities to share our life with others. Find a poem at random and you come upon Elizabeth Brewster's springtime girl who "abandoned / rubber boots too early," who is picking her way "delicately / over the small islands of mud and ice."

Open the book. Pick a poem at random. You won't go wrong.

Dr. Russ Hunt
Professor Emeritus of English, St. Thomas University
December 2016

The Story of this Book

"I set off at a sharp walk on the journey that
has not yet come to an end."

–Walter de la Mare, *Come Hither, A Collection of Rhymes
and Poems for the Young of All Ages*

Our love of children and passion for excellence in children's books, combined with our professional experience in early childhood education, informs this book. So does a friendship that goes back thirty years, when this book had its tentative beginnings as a whispery, wistful idea in an undergraduate English thesis at St. Thomas University in Fredericton, New Brunswick.

The whispers became a conversation in 1993 when we co-taught Children's Literature at St. Thomas. There we discovered a mutual appreciation of, and delight in, children's verse and poetry. We knew poetry for kids was more than cantering anapests and delightful images—but also, that even the smallest and silliest verse could be powerful in fostering language development and literacy.

We believed excellent poetry for children must also delight the parents and teachers and librarians who read to those children. As Atlantic Canadians, we had questions:

Did anyone other than us realize that Sir Charles G. D. Roberts and Bliss Carman actually penned poetry for children? Did enough people know about the beautiful lines of Labrador's Eleanor Obed, for example, or Rita Joe's collection for children, or Ken Ward's nonsense in "Mrs. Kitchen's Cats," or how a poem by Brian Bartlett and so many others could spark wonder as well as a love of poetry in children?

We asked our students, many of them teachers, what they thought poetry was and what poetry they knew from our region and concluded there was indeed a desire, and a need, for an anthology of Atlantic Canada's poetry for children that celebrated the rich poetic storytelling tradition.

Initially, our vision was to put an excellent poetry collection in the hands of children, offer a range of poetic form—from nonsense verse to free verse, from haiku to ballad to sonnet. Beginning with Sir Charles G. D. Roberts, "The Father of Canadian poetry," we would also include poems that weren't written specifically for children but ones we felt could be enjoyed by children—poems such as E. J. Pratt's "The Shark" or Elizabeth Brewster's "March Afternoon."

As we researched, we discovered there were more poems written specifically for children than we had expected. So we started there, honouring as many as we could, and worked our way to the present, searching for new voices. There are stories behind, and reasons for, every poem selected in this collection. The hardest part was stopping. Because we had too many wonderful poems in our treasure trove, we decided to limit our choices to those we felt would appeal to children of early and middle years. (Perhaps one day there will be a volume two for young adults.)

As our collection of poems grew, each one began to tell us why it belonged to Atlantic Canada. Sorting through them in one of our meetings, Sheree, unleashing her poet's word hoard, began reciting a string of words beginning with the letter W that the poems suggested to her. Anne listened. They were perfect! The words described something fundamental about us, about what it is to live in this part of the world, what ties us together:

> *Warmth*, a sense of hearth and home, of belonging;
> *Wonder*, at the dramatic natural world we live in and our place in it;
> *Weather*, which affects us directly as fishers, farmers, and woodland people;
> *Whimsy*, our undaunted sense of humour;
> *Wordplay*, the love of language tricks and the sounds of speech, perhaps a part of our rich oral traditions;
> *Whispers*, our love of tales from other worlds and other times.

We have grouped the anthology's poems under these headings because they told us to. We hope that you can hear them telling you, too.

Children's poetry, says Canadian poet Dennis Lee, "is a kind of folk art." Word music is one way to understand children's rhymes, verse, and poetry but its importance is also, we both believe, in its delivery and context. The sounds of the poems are as important as their sense, and this collection is meant to be read aloud to children. Although we know reading to children is an important part of literacy development, the shared experience goes well beyond that, stretching imaginations, tickling the senses, creating warm and comforting spaces. The literature of early childhood depends upon the human voice and a community—a community of reciters and listeners and people who care enough about children to read to them out loud and put good books into their hands.

We also know that reading to children should not stop as soon as they are able to read for themselves. As young readers develop, they continue to need to be stretched. The rich, and often surprising, vocabulary of poetry read aloud can challenge and delight. The experience of reading and sharing poetry is invaluable—in the moment of the telling of the poem there is the creation of a safe place. We need such safe places where we can be still and imagine, hear mermaids' whispers, and know how it might feel to soar like a falcon or to hold the moon in your hand.

We enter those spaces when we are part of a community that understands and cherishes the power of the written word. The poems which have chosen us speak to our inheritance as Atlantic Canadians. We want our children to treasure them, to someday share them with the children in their lives. And so, the story of this book has no ending, only new beginnings.

Anne Hunt & Sheree Fitch
May 2017

WORDALICIOUS

I devour books at breakfast,
I digest them on the bus.
I chomp through chapters at recess,
And munch whole novels for lunch.
Comics are cool, and after school
I'll polish off one or two.
But when suppertime's done, then comes the fun,
'Cause I've got reading to do!
Books are surprising and so tantalizing
I'll drool over pages for ages.
I can't get enough. It's such juicy stuff!
Action, adventure, magic, and wishes—
It's all so delectably
WORDALICIOUS!

Jennifer McGrath

Pass the Poems Please

Pass the poems please,
Pile them on my plate;
Put them right in front of me
For I can hardly wait
To taste each tangy word,
To try each tasty rhyme,
And when I've tried them once or twice
I'll try them one more time;
So, pass the poems please,
They just won't leave my head,
I have to have more poems
Before I go to bed.

Jane Baskwill

My Incredible Leanamabobber

My incredible leanamabobber
Travels wherever I go.
It's long and leans on many things,
I balance it on my toe.

I found it in the forest.
It once belonged to bears.
It's ebony with yellow spots
And great for vaulting stairs.

I lean it against the counter.
The ants march up its back.
Then slipping down the other side,
They munch their morning snack.

I lean it by my cozy bed
To poke at moaning ghosts.
And if a giant snake should hiss,
I'll jab where it hurts most.

My incredible leanamabobber
Could sail across the sea.
But maybe we'll stay home tonight
So it can lean on me.

Lynn Davies

The Joob-Joob Jungle

In the Joob-Joob jungle
Where the monkey is my uncle and
Yams grow in cans on a bubble-gum tree
I'll swish my tail
As I ride a whale
Down a river that slithers
Out to the sea.

In the Joob-Joob jungle
I can tickle my uncle who's
A monkey in funkle
While clams eat the yams
In the bubble-gum tree;
I'll stick my toes
In a hippo's nose
And somersault back
To land on a yak
And grin at the jinn
Grinning back at me

Because in Joob-Joob jungles
(where monkeys are uncles)
Things are as they please
And only as one sees
With the eye of the mind
And that's the *only* kind
Of jungle for me!

Jennifer McGrath

The Beagle and the Beluga and the Eagle's Fine Times

I know a beagle
who loved bagels
In fact he loved to beg for bagels
In fact he wagged his tail for bagels
whenever bugles blew

One day the beagle met a beluga
who played the boogie-woogie bugle
The beagle giggled, "Hi Beluga!"
then played a jig with his kazoo

Then the beagle and the beluga,
eating bagels, blowing bugles,
met a eagle who was eager
to eat some buttered bagels too

So the beagle and the eagle
and the bugle-playing beluga
sailed together and saw the
seven million
wonders of the world

It was a boondoggling
mindboggling
hornswoggling
time

They played
the Boogie-Woogie
Beluga-Eager
Eagle-Beagle
Blues

Sheree Fitch

The Bottom

Ann Livia Pluribelle
Fell one morning down a well
Fell and fell and fell and fell
Couldn't tell how far she fell
Till she hit the bottom

Ann Livia Pluribelle
Lay in bed for quite a spell
Bum in plaster like a shell
Won't be up until she's well
Cos she hit the bottom.

Ann Livia—whatsitsname
Thinks it is a bleeding shame
There is no one she can blame
Feels that all in life is rotten
Now that she has lost her bottom.

Reshard Gool

A poet swings at Christmas

for Giles Bryant

ahaa   ohoo
merrily   merrily
wingily   wingily
dingily   dingily
    o so singily

    o so singily
dingily   dongily
dongily   dingily

cheerily   beerily
    o so dearily
        a little bit wearily
    o so tearily

    o so jollily
deckily   wreckily
ivily   hallily
dollily   wallily
hollily   hollily
ringily   roundily
nightily   whitily
starily   farily

    bird in a treeily
singily   sweetily
tweetily   tweetily
wingily   dingily

merrily   merrily

   o poet so singily

upily   downily
singily   soundily

a poet swings at Christmas

Douglas Lochhead

URENTIT

Woodsplitters, tillers, trowels, salamanders,
gyprock screwguns, fertilizer spreaders,
gas-driven post hole diggers, chain wrenches,
whipper snippers, mud sucker pumps, snakes,
skill saws, chainsaws, reciprico saws,
roofracks, ramsets, routers, pop riveters,
kango cement hammers, sump pumps, sockets,
hydraulic jacks, hilti guns, sink wrenches,
flaring tools, stud finder, hack saws,
coping saws, off-set drills, disc grinders,
chimney sweepers, come-a-longs, handsaws,
car jacks, caulking guns, Coleman stoves,
mitre boxes, lawn mowers, cement drills,
picks, shovels, double bit axes, wedges,
soldering guns, glass carriers, c-clamps,
safety belts, Stillson wrench, sodcutters,
heaters, rollers, routers, and rigging.

Lesley Choyce

Little Millipede

I see a little millipede
—a silly pede
this millipede—
I see a little millipede
who floats across the sand.

She has a million skinny feet
—such mini feet
these skinny feet—
she has a million skinny feet
small waves across my hand.

She gets so scared she curls up tight
—she twirls up tight
then curls up tight—
she gets so scared she curls up tight
I place her on the sand.

Gretchen Kelbaugh

Mrs. Kitchen's Cats

Mrs. Kitchen's cats
      don't wear no funny hats
      they speak Chinese
      to all their fleas
      and what's the use of that

Mrs. Kitchen's cats
      wear socks and shoes with spats
      they use the phone
      when she's not home
      they love long feline chats

Mrs. Kitchen's cats
      sleep on wrestling mats
      they romp and roll
      to Nat King Cole
      then drive her car with flats

Mrs. Kitchen's cats
      play tag with cricket bats
      they move the couch
      in search of mouse
      to eat with beans and rats

Ken Ward

The Platypus

The platypus was designed
for life in the water
she looks like a duck
but swims like an otter.

Ken Ward

Uncle Tom

Uncle Tom
was an old tom cod.
He travelled far
and wide.
He went down
on the Labrador
to find himself
a bride.

He swam as far
as Hopedale.
He swam right down
to Nain.

And then he turned
himself around
and swam
back home again.

Al Pittman

Young Clem Clam

Young Clem Clam
thought as he swam
as clumsy
as ever he could.

How he did wish
he was shaped
like a fish
and could swim
wherever he would.

Al Pittman

Here, then Gone

I dip and I dance
over water and land.
I dart, then glance
my jewels at you.

    My eyes are huge,
    incredibly wide,
    I see above me,
    and side to side.

        I munch up bees,
        butterflies too.
        Flies are delightful,
        a mosquito will do.

            On my four long wings
            that flash in the sun,
            I'm here, then gone,
            my hunting's done.

                What am I?

Lynn Davies

Unsnarling String
X

If every snarl has seven snarls
and each of those snarls has seven more
and each of those in turn has seven
and those seven, seven
and those seven, seven each
how many snarls in all?

Answer: One.

William Bauer

Unfinished

Think of what you want to say and say it.
Pick up what you want to play and play it.
Imagine how you want to live and live it.
Find out what you have to give and give it.
Think of what you want to see and see it.
Dream of what you want to be and

Zach Hapeman

Weather

Yesterday's Storm

The elephants trumpeted
Squealing like pigs
In a sky full of muck
And of feathers and twigs.
Their great feet got stuck
In the crotches of trees
And they tangled in power lines
Up to their knees.
They sounded like furniture movers
And freight trains.

And out of their trunks
Spewed the angry gray rains.
Today it is quiet. The wind stopped at dawn
And we sighed with relief
That the beasts had all gone.

Ferne Peake

Typhoon Alice

Today's the day I wear bags in my boots,
my leaky boots, my worn out boots.
Today's the day I stuff bags in my boots,
because of Typhoon Alice.

She pounded up the coast last night,
churned the fish with all her might,
washed our roads, flicked out lights,
while I was in pyjamas.

Up and down our street she howled,
kicked up gravel, spit and growled,
In and out of dreams she prowled,
while I was trying to sleep.

She ripped up roots and battered trees,
flattened plants and scissored leaves,
created rivers as she pleased,
Ms. Turbulous Typhoon Alice.

Today's the day I wear bags in my boots,
my leaky boots, my worn out boots.
I'll splash down streets with holes in my boots.
Thank you, Typhoon Alice!

Lynn Davies

Port Elgin Evening

The Gaspereau River
open this cold
March evening
plates of ice
littering shoreline
brown marsh grass
wheezing
near an old fort
silent with history
butting the bay
near Indian Point
where ducks bob
feathers against chill
spruce and bare maples
rocking in wind
waves impatient
as evening settles
lights flickering
in the distance

Doug Underhill

North Dance

Dance sea
on dark cliff
hard and high;
dance gull
in sea salt
shaking sky.
Dance spruce
in forest
black and tight;
dance day
with long leaps
in the night.
Dance fly
in tiny,
spitting swarm;
dance melt
down mountain
in the warm.
Dance frost on berries
ripened low;
dance wind
with cold and
cold with snow.

Ellen Bryan Obed

Sky Carver

Gently the sun
with steady eye
whittled at winter
from the sky.

Deeper she cut
with sharpened ray
as pieces of winter
fell away.

Warmly she held
it up when done,

"This is my carving
called Spring,"
said the Sun.

Ellen Bryan Obed

March Afternoon

Suddenly it is spring
and cars come splashing
rivers of mud and water
while people walking leap
over rippling puddles
balance on ice and slime.

Brown snow melts,
mixed with candy wrappers,
last year's leaves
cigarette butts
and crushed red berries.

And overhead the sky softens
is a polar blue
tepid
where one cloud floats.

Coats are unbuttoned
Scarves thrust into pockets
And there—one girl who abandoned
rubber boots too early
picks her way delicately
over the small islands of mud and ice.

Elizabeth Brewster

An April Morning

Once more in misted April
The world is growing green.
Along the winding river
The plumey willows lean.

Beyond the sweeping meadows
The looming mountains rise,
Like battlements of dreamland
Against the brooding skies.

In every wooded valley
The buds are breaking through,
As though the heart of all things
No languor ever knew.

The golden-wings and bluebirds
Call to their heavenly choirs.
The pines are blued and drifted
With smoke of brushwood fires.

And in my sister's garden
Where little breezes run,
The golden daffodillies
Are blowing in the sun.

Bliss Carman

The Flute of Spring

I know a shining meadow stream
That winds beneath an Eastern hill,
And all year long in sun or gloom
Its murmuring voice is never still.

The summer dies more gently there,
The April flowers are earlier,
The first warm rain-wind from the Sound
Sets all their eager hearts astir.

And there when lengthening twilights fall
As softly as a wild bird's wing,
Across the valley in the dusk
I hear the silver flute of spring.

Bliss Carman

Annapolis Valley

I was born in fairyland,
The Valley, in the spring,
When all along her winding roads
The trees were blossoming.

Ah, then upon my upturned face
A petal fluttered down,
A bit of pastel velvet
Clipped from a fairy gown.

Now once again the seasons change
The birds begin to sing
And would that I were there to see
The Valley, blossoming.

Joyce Barkhouse

From *Lasso the Wind*

New leaves! New leaves!
Spring is busy
Greening earth's eaves.
Brooks go dizzy;
Robins delight.
Everything's green
That once was white.
Butterflies preen;
Gilt lilies flute.
All blossoms sing,
Now rain takes root.
Each queen and king
Slow promenades,
In skirts and pants
Cross dales and glades,
Where sunbeams dance
On wings and webs,
And little green sleeves,
While chill air ebbs
To leaves, new leaves!

George Elliott Clarke

May

Here is the merry month of May
With a heigh heigh ho and a laddie O.
I can leave off my coat when I romp and play
As I hop o'er the hills to meet my daddy O.

O I'll let the winds blow through my hair
With a heigh heigh ho and a laddie O,
And the soft rain splash on my arm all bare,
He says I can, does my daddy O.

O a mayflower pink will I carry home
With a heigh heigh ho and a laddie O,
I'm a great big man now going far to roam
For I'm sitting on the shoulders of my daddy O.

Helen Creighton

A Wake-Up Song

Sun's up; wind's up! Wake up, dearies!
      Leave your coverlets white and downy,
June's come into the world this morning.
      Wake up, Golden Head! Wake up, Brownie!

Dew on the meadow-grass, waves on the water,
      Robins in the rowan-tree wondering about you!
Don't keep the buttercups so long waiting.
      Don't keep the bobolinks singing without you.

Wake up, Golden Head! Wake up, Brownie!
      Cat-bird wants you in the garden soon.
You and I, butterflies, bobolinks, and clover,
      We've a lot to do on the first of June.

Sir Charles G. D. Roberts

Just Summer

When the sun pours down like honey
and melts in puddles on the road,
when the warm breeze that's blowing
seems to lighten every load
that's just summer 'round here.

The trees are heavy laden
and the earth smells spicy sweet.
All of creation has spilled out on the street.
That's just summer 'round here,
just summer 'round here.

There's laughter on the corners
and there's music in the air.
Endless possibilities are hiding everywhere.
That's just summer 'round here,
just summer 'round here.

That sudden brief explosion
of energy and sun
is bittersweet and over,
as soon as it's begun.

So while the sun is shining
come and dance along with me.
It's only for a moment,
close your eyes and you will see
just summer 'round here,
just summer 'round here.

Jennifer Wyatt

Spinning Wheel Song

When safely the harvest is stored in the barn,
    'Tis then we make ready for spinning the yarn;
When summer is over and winter is near,
    The song of the wheel is the sound that you hear.
    Oh, this is the song that the spinning wheel sings:
    "You soon will need mufflers and mittens and things,
    So draw a long thread with each turn of the wheel
    And double and twist it with spindle and reel!"

When flowers are faded and swallows are fled
    And trees on the hillsides are yellow and red.
When mornings are frosty and evenings are long,
    'Tis then we will sing you our spinning wheel song.
    Oh, this is the song that the spinning wheel sings:
    "You soon will need mufflers and mittens and things,
    So draw a long thread with each turn of the wheel
    And double and twist it with spindle and reel!"

Soon over the mountains the snowdrifts will come,
    And settle down deep by the door of our home.
With mufflers and mittens, how warm we shall feel
    And value the yarn that was spun on the wheel.
    Oh, this is the song that the spinning wheel sings:
    "You soon will need mufflers and mittens and things,
    So draw a long thread with each turn of the wheel
    And double and twist it with spindle and reel!"

Grace Helen Mowat

November

The blue-jays squeal: "More rain! More rain!"
The sky's all blotch and stain.
The colours of Earth are melted down
To dark spruce green and dull grass brown.

Black ducks, last week, held parliament
Up-river there…Gulls came and went.
Now that they're gone, nor'wester blown,
The grim gulls wheel and bob alone.

Nary a leaf has kept its hold.
The thicket's naked, black and cold.
Then zig-zag, like a skating clown,
The first white flake comes down.

Milton Acorn

The Saint John in Winter

That grand old river, the Saint John,
Has closed her weary eyes;
She's put her winter blankets on,
Now all tucked in she lies.

And what cares she if nights are cold,
Or if wintery winds do blow?
She's warm and snug on her river bed,
'Neath her blankets of ice and snow.

So peacefully she'll slumber on
'Til the warm, glad days of spring;
When kissed by the sun's warm rays,
She'll awake again and sing.

Then merrily she'll travel on,
Through wooded hill and lea,
'Til once again, with a glad rush
She joins her mate, the sea.

Vella Pearl Aiton

The Winter Yard

Bundled,

eyes watering against the glare,

we wade

into the crusty winter yard.

Bushes hang heavy

with suet-soaked onion bags,

pine cones drip peanut butter and seeds.

Coconuts hang by theirs eyes

and Javex bottles swing crazy

on the clothesline.

We smile

red tight

and closed with cold

and retreat to wait.

Shoulder to shoulder with cat at the window,

noses pressed on fogged-up glass,

we watch,

impatient.

Erin calls,

"Birds! Come here! We have seeds for you!"

Gulls sweep the sky,

starlings crowd the neighbouring maples.

Jays scream.

Hundreds of wings beat the air,
and
        then
                they
                        descend.

Norene Smiley

Frozen Freedom

Playing forward
leaning hard
I piston straight toward the puck.

The slice of my blades
hiss across the ice
as if I've strapped on a pair of frozen steel blue snakes

Fine scars and tracks cut and groove behind me
crossed and recrossed and crossed out
by the Zamboni's hushing erasure

The crowd is a shouting blur
the rink is as wide as a white frozen sea
and I am nothing more than a pair of skates and a stick

The rink chill
novocaines my teeth
in a perma-frozen grin

I am puck, stick, ice, goal, and crowd
a blink of lonely starlit heaven moment
grinning, giggling, a blizzard of fun.

Steve Vernon

Three Ways to Remember Winter

I.
wavelap on snowtoast wintercrust
sunribbon razorblue skyrip sting of winter
oceanedge cityfeet shuffle saltsand
and gentlekick icesilver slivers of ice and rock
pebble and shell back to sea
from beachbreak bib of tide and time

II.
gullrip sound of wing and beak
backing down the windwhip
fearstruck from inland man
wading gundeath on saltmarsh squadron
bulletready to retrieve light
from the eye of neverready skyswimmers

II.
tidal water of seastilled level sand
salt sidewalk for city footslap
of boots that break and break and begin again
rubberfoot slap on sea and sand
easypaced miracle of manwalk
twofoot parade of mammal legs
lifeblood thump of saltblood seeker.

Lesley Choyce

Wonder

The Dragon Tree

Strange-scented birds and song-flowers grow
In the garden where I cannot go,
Where green-trunked trees grey apples hold
And blue fish swim in pools of gold.

And always there a green sun glows
To burn the song of the red-leafed rose,
While yellow grasses bend their knees
Before a bluebird-smelling breeze.

Around the garden's circle flies
The dragon-tree to eat the skies
With silver-scented fruit that sings
Hid in the branches of his wings.

That garden now to me is gone
Where sight and sound and sense are one,
But children walk there still before
They eat the dragon's cherished store.

Fred Cogswell

Full Circle

A little boy holds one end of a string.
The other end is tied to his pull-toy.
The pull-toy's wheels rest on the grass.
The grass is rooted in the earth.
The earth touches the water of the sea.
The sunlight strikes the water and draws it up.
The water vaporized becomes a cloud.
The cloud bursts and falls as rain.
The rain falls on the little boy holding a string.

Fred Cogswell

Her eyes on the Horizon

What a coincidence
our firmament fixtures
(permanent pictures, sources of light)
are roughly the shape of our sources of sight.
I can't solve this riddle, but sorcerers might,
and I can't help but think
as I stand at the brink
of the sea with a shell at my ear that the shell
(which appears to my sources of sight like an ear)
might be hearing the sound of the ocean as well...
Which is sea? Which is shell? Which is ear? I can't tell,
and I won't even think on the subject of smell,
which leads to the subject of breathing out here,
on the brink of
what I think of
as the sea.

Kathleen Winter

From *Lasso the Wind*

The ocean's a lot of brittle foam
That makes to stay, but makes no home.
It looks like marble under light,
Or suave velvet set soaking wet.
I like the salt it leaves once dry—
As spice from Greece or Italy—
Or how it coddles when I swim,
And bounces every buoyant limb.
I think it's better than the sky
Because it's closer—motherly—
And keeps us clean as spotless priests
And sinks dead-weight philosophies.

Waves whittle the horizon down
Until the sun descends to drown.

George Elliott Clarke

The Bay of Fundy

I like the Bay of Fundy,
Where tides creep up the strand,
With driftwood for the fire,
And rockweed for the land.
From Yarmouth to Chignecto, around and back again,
They reach the Quoddy Islands and wash the shores of Maine.

I like the Bay of Fundy,
Where sandstone islands wait
The rosy kiss of sunset,
Beside the western gate.
And up the inland rivers, that seek the Fundy tides,
A pleasant land of apple trees and happy homes abides.

I like the Bay of Fundy—
For when the tide is out,
So many wonders of the deep
Are scattered all about.
Oh, happy Bay of Fundy; for there forevermore,
Children find their fairy lands beside its lovely shore!

Grace Helen Mowat

From *Where the Wind Sleeps*

"It's dark out there. I can't see the wind."

> —"You never see the wind.
> You only see what the wind touches."

"The wind must be tired from pounding so long. It must be hungry."

> —"The wind isn't hungry.
> It grabs fruits and nuts
> from trees. It gobbles
> berries and mushrooms.
> Sometimes it munches
> leaves. I've even seen the
> wind eat sand. But I don't
> know where it sleeps when
> it's tired."

"I know. It dives into the water and sleeps on the bottom of the ocean. Or maybe it sleeps in the…"

> —"Shhh. Did you hear that?"

"What?"

> —"The wind just kicked over the garbage can."

"No. The wind was swinging on the rusty gate."

> —"Remember when we were walking to school and
> the wind was so strong it almost knocked you down?"

"Yes. And in the summer the wind took our kites high in the air. And it was gentle and blew through my hair."

—"That was a breeze. A breeze is the wind's baby."

"Listen…"

—"What?"

"I hear the wind whistling through a hole in the bird house, whoo whoo whoo whoo."

—"I hear it clanging the chimes."

"Is the wind lonely?"

—"No. It brushes cobwebs out of the grass. It shakes trees. It dives into water and makes waves go up, up, up. It loves these things."

"But where does it sleep?"

—"Maybe in cars when people go inside their houses. Our car is always cold in the morning."

"Listen. Do you hear that?"

—"I hear a ping, ping, ping, ping, ping."

"That's the rain
It's dancing on the roof with the wind.
And the wind is dancing in the woods with the trees."

—"Sometimes a little bit of the wind gets into people."

"How do you know?"

>—"I know the wind is in me
>when I feel like running
>very fast through the grass
>or jumping in puddles
>or hugging someone."

"Does the wind hug?"

>—"Yes, the wind hugs the clouds and
>carries them across the sky.
>When birds fly the wind
>lifts them."

Carole Glasser Langille

St. John's Haiku

a bronze-lettered plaque,
oil tanks ice-rimed—
headland dragons sleep

round the bowl of the harbour
ships' horns ricochet—
a skein of gulls wheels.

cars bumper to bumper,
headed for the cove:
beached caplin roiling.

shattered concrete step:
dock unfurls its frills in cracks—
ship clears the Narrows.

Mary Dalton

A Boy, A Tree, A Turtle Said

A little boy who sat reading
In his sunny window said,
Suddenly to himself said,
And to the mulberry tree in the yard
With the gift of the sun in its leaves,
And to the turtle in the water jungle
On the sunny windowsill,
"There is no one like me in the whole wide world!"

And the mulberry tree in the yard,
With the gift of sun in its leaves,
Said right back to the boy
In the sunny window nook,
"There is no green tree like me in the world!"
The mulberry tree said.
"No tree like me in the whole wide world!"
This is what the mulberry said.

And the turtle from his water jungle
In the sunny window said
To the mulberry tree and the boy,
"There is no turtle like me in the whole wide world,
Not in the whole wide world!" he said.
"No turtle like me, like me!"
Is what the turtle said.

But did the little boy hear
What the mulberry tree and the turtle said?
Or did the strangeness of being himself
And nobody else in the whole wide world
Make such a hurdy-gurdy sound in his head
That he heard only it
And not what the mulberry tree
And what the turtle said?

Kay Smith

Through Dark Trees I See the River

Through dark trees I see the river.
Autumn leaves glow
Turning in black water.

All day long the soft rain falls
As I cast at Fraser's Pool.
In the afternoon a salmon leaped
just where the bubbles and the little flecks of foam
slowed out on the black water.
I cast there
and had a strike
And on the third cast after that
my line tightened.   I felt its weight
And then it was gone.

Great silver sided might have been
Bearing all my might have beens
Swim in your dark caverns
While I watch the rain
And the tamaracks, yellow against the dark spruce,
Receding down the Nashwaak Valley.

Theodore Colson

A Feline Silhouette

They faced each other, taut and still;
Arched hickory, neck and spine;
Heads down, tails straight, with hair of quill,
The fence—the battleline

The slits within their eyes describe
The nature of their feud;
Each came to represent a tribe
Which never was subdued.

One minute just before they fought,
Before their blood called—"time,"
One told the other what he thought
In words I cannot rhyme

They hit each other in mid-air
In one terrific bound,
And even yet, as I'm aware
They have not struck the ground.

E. J. Pratt

The Shark

He seemed to know the harbour,
So leisurely he swam;
His fin,
Like a piece of sheet-iron,
Three-cornered,
And with knife-edge,
Stirred not a bubble
As it moved
With its base-line on the water.

His body was tubular
And tapered
And smoke-blue,
And as he passed the wharf
He turned,
And snapped at a flat-fish
That was dead and floating.
And I saw the flash of a white throat,
And a double row of white teeth,
And eyes of metallic grey,
Hard and narrow and slit.

Then out of the harbour,
With that three-cornered fin,
Shearing without a bubble the water
Lithely,
Leisurely,
He swam—
That strange fish,
Tubular, tapered, smoke-blue
Part vulture, part wolf,
Part neither—for his blood was cold.

E. J. Pratt

Falcon on a Dark Day

falcon! chasing clouds
that the thousandth man
of a thousand men

on each other's shoulders
could not reach.
falcon! even quicker up there

than you seem down here
where sharp-topped pines
cut sub-zero winds.

no hood or bells on you.
no talons twisted
to the shape of a gloved hand.

i do not even see
patterned face or smooth throat
or yellow irises

or legs tucked under
or that blood-pumping heart
beating quick

quicker than my heart beats.
all i see is
motion and silhouette

merged into one.
the air inside those
hundreds of hollow bones

as visible as
beak or tongue or underbelly.
if i see wings

i see just wings
stark against grey clouds
and not feathers

full enough to plume arrows
that haul other silhouettes
out of the sky.

falcon! chasing clouds
that the thousandth man
of a thousand men

on each other's shoulders
could not reach.
you are the one

who makes me walk on
when you slip into pines.
who tempts me to say

"falcons do not fly
because they have wings—
falcons have wings

because they fly"

Brian Bartlett

Black Cat

Black cat
in a white alley
is like you
isn't it:
quietly padding the snow
between tense red walls
all the strangers watching
—such harsh looks.

Christopher Heide

Three Tulips Stand and Talk to Me

Three tulips stand and talk to me.
One is as yellow as can be,
one red, another purple black.
I hear but cannot answer back;
the things they tell me are so true,
such things there is no answer to.
They say to be a tulip one
must bed in soil, must burn in sun,
must brood in blackness, swell with rain,
must stumble through the earth in pain
from frosty night to flaming song,
to joy that lasts not overlong
in measured time, although they say
no moment ends in tulip day.
To earth they drain their cup of thanks
for broken light in crowded ranks.
They drink the sun to give it back
in yellow, red, and purple black.

Kenneth Leslie

The Saw Bug's Toil

A sparrow flutters to the grass to peck for seeds and insects.
The saw bug tows leaves through soil and twigs.
The sparrow stalks the bug lost in a
web of stems, leaves, buds, flowers, and vines.

Heddy Johannesen

Rhubarb

Long the fishing place abandoned,
Long the houses grey and still,
Long the gravestones dim and leaning,
But the rhubarb by the hill
Straight and high as if the pickers
Soon would pull the stalks aside—
Some for sauce and some for puddings,
Some for summer supper pies.

Ellen Bryan Obed

Buttercups

Like showers of gold dust on the marsh,
Or an inverted sky,
The buttercups are dancing now
Where silver brooks run by.
Bright, bright,
As fallen flakes of light,
They nod
In time to every breeze
That chases shadows swiftly lost
Amid those grassy seas.
See, what a golden frenzy flies
Through the light-hearted flowers!
In mimic fear they flutter now;
Each fairy blossom cowers.
Then up, then up,
Each shakes its yellow cup
And nods
In careless grace once more—
A very flood of sunshine seems
Across the marsh to pour.

L. M. Montgomery

Concert in the Forest

There is a concert in the forest
as the sun goes down;
but we don't make a noise
not one little sound.

The wind blows the leaves
into whispers on the trees;
the soft summer grasses
make a hissing in the breeze.

But we don't make a noise,
not one little sound
when the forest concert starts
as the sun goes down.

The crickets chirp good night
in voices clear and high;
the owl softly hoots
while the moon climbs the sky.

But we don't make a noise,
not one little sound
when the forest concert starts
as the sun goes down.

The stream adds a babble
to the bullfrogs as they boom
and in the still dark pond
a lily folds its bloom.

But we don't make a noise,
not one little sound
when the forest concert starts
as the sun goes down.

The bees drone a buzz
as they heavy-laden go
to their hive in the tree
and the sound is deep and low.

But we don't make a noise,
not one little sound
when the forest concert starts
as the sun goes down.

The loon sends her cry
with the cawing of the crows;
coyotes blend their howls
with the choir as it grows.

But we don't make a noise,
not one little sound
when the forest concert starts
as the sun goes down.

The squirrels chitter, chatter
and tree frogs pipe their peeps;
fireflies spread the news—
this is no time to sleep.

But we don't make a noise,
not one little sound
when the forest concert starts
as the sun goes down.

Like threads upon a loom,
the notes sweet and strong
weave a tapestry of music
from the choir and the song.

Now we don't make a noise
not one little sound;
while we listen to the concert
as the sun goes down.

Joanne LeBlanc-Haley

What Can I Do for the World Today?

What can I do for the world, today?
I can spread the news
to reduce
to recycle
and re-use.

What can I do for the world today?
I can re-sole, re-use
repair my shoes.

What can I do for the world today?
Start a green-thumb club,
build a backyard compost,
then when you boil an egg or eat an orange
toss in the peel and stuff.

What can I do for the world today?
Not litter.
Not waste.
Not destroy marshlands and tidepools.

What can I do for the world today?
Lots!
What can you do?

Maxine Tynes

Whimsy

In the Garden

"When I die
I'll grow wings
And fly.
        Don't grin."

Said the caterpillar,
Crawling by.

Alden Nowlan

Wet Feet

A very funny summer clown
joined a parade in Charlottetown.
She had two funny floppy feet
which got all wet on Water Street.

Hugh MacDonald

Toes

I counted all my toes
and two of them were missing.
Where they are, who knows
But likely somewhere kissing.

Hugh MacDonald

Dead Man's Pond

We liked to play
in Victoria Park
but we'd run home
before it got dark.
The spirits woke
and stretched and yawned
then they stepped out
of Dead Man's Pond.
But we'd be home
in bed by then.
Tomorrow we'd
run back again.

Hugh MacDonald

Hot Foot

He loved the sizzling summer heat
and burned the bottoms of his feet.
The road was like a frying pan
each toe a tiny sausage man.
And every night he liked to dream
of squishing toes through soft ice cream.

Hugh MacDonald

The Balloon Man

The Balloon Man had the hiccups
One wild and windy day;
And every time he hiccupped
A balloon would get away.

He hiccuped hard.
He hiccuped long.
And when the day was done;
The sky had all the bright balloons
And he had not a one!

Shirley Downey

A Gommil From Bumble Bee Bight

An octopus down in Old Shop
Was snoozing on top of a lop,
When an iceberg so white
Sidled by in the night
And froze him into a full stop.

A lad who lived out in Monroe
Grew a fabulous wart on his toe
But on Bonfire Night
He set it alight
That luminous lad from Monroe.

Tom Dawe

Reuben Rat

Reuben Rat was such a brat.
He lived behind the laundromat.
When ladies came to do their wash,
Cleaning clothes with swishy-swosh,
He'd jump upon their calicos
With muddy, little, ratty toes.

Reuben Rat was such a brat.
He liked to tease the village cat,
Who always took a morning stroll,
Twitching tail on purr patrol.
He'd jump upon the kitty's back:
A sudden, daring, rat attack.

Reuben Rat was such a brat.
He stole the farmer's old straw hat.
Farmer Hoyt had set it down
To wipe the sweat from crinkled crown.
This became the rodent's home:
A sweaty, stained, and tattered dome.

Reuben Rat was such a brat.
He ate and ate and got so fat,
A berry here, banana there,
The Farmers' Market summer fare.
This brought an end to Reuben's fun.
He could not hide from anyone!

He could not jump on calicos
With muddy, little ratty toes.

He could not jump on kitty's back
In a daring rat attack.
He could not steal the farmer's hat
With sweaty stains and tattered tats.

That bratty little Reuben Rat!

Kim McAdam

Merman Ben

Ben is a merman, long and lean
under the sea with his shimmering beam of a smile
and a tail that goes splish and goes splash
with no mind for the news or the market crash.

He flosses his teeth with a jellyfish stinger
he has a doorbell but no need to ring'er
his house is wide open, for everyone
octopus, squid: come on over for fun!

Seaweed sandwich with eel in the middle
'cause eels have a habit of unwanted piddles.
"Just joshin'," says he to the tremblin' snakes,
"I like crumbles and crispers and cakes.
A kelp-e-tarian's what I am: I eat what can't walk,
      and not what can talk
that's how I stay so slick and so lean
and keep friends who have gills and baleen.
I won't eat him and I won't eat you."

(PHEW!)

Nobody's faster than Merman Ben
with his fins and his flicks flicking again
to propel him through current and rising tide
missed by all but the keenly eyed
who see distant leaps and mysterious bubbles
at coves and beaches and seaside puddles.

When you're down and you're out with the market crash
the worldwide news and the bang and smash
go out to the ocean and stand by the shore
and see a few things that mermen adore.

Rolling swell that spills into pools
the sun through fathoms and glittering jewels
shipwreck-reation and foamy surf
and wave from the grasses and sandy turf.

Kate Inglis

At The Blue Moo Confectionary Store

I had only one dirty nickel
so I bought squishy molasses kisses
and dreamed of Big Candy Land
where houses are peanut brittle
and trees with wintergreen leaves
grow giant taffy apples
the roads are smooth rock candy
with barley sugar cars
and clouds of pink cotton candy
rain delicious flavours of pop.

People are all-the-way-lickable
in Big Candy
whether vanilla, lemon, cherry, and chocolate
their lips are tutti-frutti
their teeth are peppermint
life is lollypops and marshmallows
but till that day when the Holy cow
comes to carry us to Big Candy
I dream and chew my nickel's worth
at the Blue Moo Confectionary Store.

Ed Yeomans

Eating

I don't enjoy my meal today.
I wish my mom would go away—
For not too long—an hour or two—
At least until this meal is through.

She's telling me I chew too fast,
And says the meal should last and last.
She's wanting me to sit up straight,
And keep my elbows off the plate.

She points to cabbage on my chin,
And says the place for food is IN.
To gulp is bad and so are slurps,
And no one ever, ever burps.

She doesn't know it's hard for boys
To eat their food without a noise.
I think until I'm old and big,
I'd really like to be a pig.

A piglet's mom cares not a hoot
If crumbs are sprinkled on his snoot.
And if he drops
His slippery slops,
She even finds it rather cute.

She lets him gobble up his meal;
(She knows *exactly* how I feel),
For when he slurps,
She simply burps,
And guzzles down an orange peel.

He lets his shoulders sag and droop,
And when he's eating up his goop,
Without a Please,
He lifts his knees,
And puts his ankles in his soup.

For even if a pig is big,
He loves to take his snout and dig;
He slavers, slops, and gloops and glops.
I'd love, just LOVE to be a pig.

Budge Wilson

On Etiquette Day

On Etiquette Day
a band doesn't play
and the street isn't decked out with banners.
The sun hides away
and the children can't play
and everyone thinks about manners.
But they pin (with loud laughter)
tails (the day after)
on the organizational planners.

Kathleen Winter

But I Don't Like Peas

I'm sitting down to supper.
I wonder what we'll have?
My mother is a capital cook!
That makes me giggly glad.
She cooks a roasted chicken.
It's juicy, crisp, and sweet.
At least, that's what my Daddy says,
BUT I DON'T LIKE MEAT!

I hear the kettle boiling.
My sister makes some tea.
Of course, that's what the big ones drink.
I know it's not for me.
If I drink this other stuff,
Strong bones in me are built.
It soothes my uncle's ulcer well,
BUT I DON'T LIKE MILK!

There's always mashed potatoes,
Or fried, or baked, or creamed.
You know, I thought I ate one once,
But it was just a dream.
My Grammy says green vegetables
Are extra good for me.
My brother eats them from the pod,
BUT I DON'T LIKE PEAS!

Now, every kid likes chocolate,
Thick and sweet and brown.
Every time my finger dips,
My mother makes a frown!
My aunt gives me an apple,
And tells me that I'm cute.
I guess I am good-looking,
BUT I DON'T LIKE FRUIT!

My family will not listen.
There's something on the shelf.
You spread it on some buttered bread.
Make it easy on yourself!
I cannot get my point across.
I'm in a fix. I am.
They say: "Please eat your supper, Bill.
You can't have bread and jam!"

Kim McAdam

Tantrum Poems
III

No one can make me swallow this piece of meat
You can take me to the circus but you can't
Make me like it and you can buy me
Pink cotton candy but so what I
Have not yet swallowed this piece of meat
And I could join the freak show and
Come to be the little boy who grew up
Fed out of tubes and bottles and held
A piece of meat in his mouth for
Thirty-five years and everyone
Will say and won't I be glad when they do
What cruel parents he must have had
To drive him to do such a thing as that

William Bauer

The Whale and the Frog

Said the Monarch of the seas to the frog in the hole,
"I wallow where I please, from Equator to the Pole;
I swallow ships' knees
and the world remarks my sneeze
and the fishes heed my wishes where the green waters roll."
"Just to think!" said the frog in the hole.

"From the Carolina Islands to the Tides of Fundy Bay
I dash and I splash with a mighty careless motion.
Every billow knows my sway when with hurricanes I play
as I roll to my goal," said the Monarch of the Ocean.
The frog's reply was droll, "Why I didn't have a notion!"

"Come, leave your shallow pool!
Learn in a deeper school!
Expand your ego with imperial pride!
The sun has never set on my kingdom of the wet!
Hop on my back, I'll take you for a ride!"
Said the frog, "Your back is slippery
And your mouth is very wide!"

His Majesty grew mighty wroth
and churned the ocean to a froth
and spit and swore, "If I could walk
I'd come ashore and *then* we'd talk!"

He sneezed and bellowed as he went,
"I don't believe in argument!"
But just as if he hadn't gone
the frog politely whispered on:

"Dreaming on this lily pad since I was a tiny tad,
news I do not often see of your liquid monarchy;

for your capers in the papers, where you wallow,
whom you swallow,
I have had no time to read,
strumming tunes on my guitar
which is more engrossing far
than a monarch's bloody deed!
Just what does it avail when you flail with your tail?
Can the blue be any bluer for your trouble?
Is the rainbow in the sky and grander though more high

than the rainbow I espy within a bubble?

All the beauty ever known in this shallow pool is sown,
here the candle-moths flicker in the twilight glow,
the pine's sable plume nods above its shadow gloom,
and its visitors are stars, I'd have you know!"

Kenneth Leslie

Lukey's Boat

Lukey's boat is painted green, aha my boys,
Lukey's boat is painted green,
The prettiest little boat you ever seen.
Aha me boys a riddle I day.

Lukey's boat got a fine fore cutty, aha my boys,
Lukey's boat got a fine fore cutty,
And every seam is chinked with putty.
Aha me boys a riddle I day.

Lukey's boat got high stop sails, aha my boys,
Lukey's boat got high stop sails,
And she was planched with copper nails.
Aha me boys a riddle I day.

Oh, Lukey's boat got a high stopped jib, aha my boys,
Oh, Lukey's boat got a high stopped jib
And a patent block to her foremast head,
Aha me boys a riddle I day.

I think, says Lukey, I'll make her bigger, aha my boys,
I think, says Lukey, I'll make her bigger,
I'll load her down with a one-claw jigger.
Aha me boys a riddle I day.

Lukey's rolling out his grub, aha my boys,
Lukey's rolling out his grub,
One split pea in a ten-pound tub.
Aha me boys a riddle I day.

Oh, Lukey he sailed down the shore, aha my boys,
Oh, Lukey he sailed down the shore
to catch some fish from Labrador,
Aha me boys a riddle I day.

Aha, says Lukey, the blinds are down, aha my boys,
Aha, says Lukey, the blinds are down,
My wife is dead and underground.
Aha me boys a riddle I day.

Aha, says Lukey, I don't care, aha my boys,
Aha, says Lukey, I don't care,
I'll get me another in the spring of the year.
Aha me boys a riddle I day.

Attributed to Virtue Keen

Halifax Boys

Five little boys from Halifax
Were playing on the shore,
When one of them for home "made tracks"
And then there were but four.

Four little boys from Halifax
Were chopping down a tree,
When one went home to grind his axe
And then there were but three.

Three little boys from Halifax
With cold were looking blue,
One went home for some warm socks
And then there were but two.

Two little boys from Halifax
Were firing off a gun,
When one went home all full of cracks
And this left only one.

One little boy from Halifax
Was playing with a ball,
It bounced and gave him such hard whacks
There was no boy at all.

Unknown

Note: This poem was originally published anonymously. Although there is no date of publication, this poem was dedicated to King Edward VII and Queen Alexandra of England, who reigned from 1901 to 1910.

Once Upon a Pine Tree

Once upon a pine tree there was a little gnome,
He found his tree some time ago and made it his home.
Every single morning he sips his chestnut tea,
And then he takes all afternoon to tidy up his tree.
Then falls the evening; the sun begins to set.
The little gnome goes fishing with his special fishing net.
Then he cooks his dinner with a little berry topping.
He eats and eats 'til he can no more and his tummy feels like popping.
The moon and her star daughters begin to shine so bright.
That's when the gnomie knows it's time for him to say good night.
He climbs the wooden stairs—turns off the mossy light,
Then says his prayers, winks at the moon, and pulls his covers tight.

Hallie Rose Mazurkiewicz

The Piper and the Chiming Peas

There was a little piper man
As merry as you please,
Who heard one day the sweet-pea blossoms
Chiming in the breeze.

He murmured with a courtly grace
That set them quite at ease,
"I never knew that you had such
accomplishments as these!

"If I should pipe until you're ripe
I think that by degrees
You might become as wise as I
And chime in Wagnerese!"

"Oh, no, kind sir! That could not be!"
replied the modest peas.
"We only play such simple airs
as suit the bumblebees."

Sir Charles G. D. Roberts

Street Cleaning

City men
sweeping the street
outside my apartment

one leans on his broom
eyes roaming
checking

then when he thinks
no one's looking
bends low
edges his hand
under the curb
lifts
holds the sidewalk up
with his one hand
and with the other
gathers up a pile of leaves
and sweeps them
under.

Al Pittman

In Grandma's Attic

Up in Grandma's attic
I found a great old trunk;
She says there's not much in it,
She says it's full of junk;
But I know what Grandma doesn't,
It's full of magic things;
Like hero's hats, and kingly jewels,
And drapes for fairy's wings;
I think I'll keep it a secret,
Between just you and me,
When we dress up together,
Just think what we can be!

Jane Baskwill

Warmth

Canada Home

Some homes are where flowers forever blow,
The sun shining hotly the whole year round;
But our Home glistens with six months of snow,
Where frost without wind heightens every sound,
And Home is Home wherever it is,
When we are together and nothing amiss.

Juliana Horatia Ewing

Untitled

At age seven
To Springhill Junction we came,
My father and I
And sister Annabel.

There we made our home
Of birchbark and pole
And a bed of pine branches.
I remember its comfort.

This was my home.
A memory stands out—
A wigwam high on the hill
In nineteen thirty-eight.

Rita Joe

View from Window

My small clean room has pink wallpaper
The bed is high and white
On a ledge above the window
are six books
and a model of a sailing ship

In the backyard
one hen wanders through grass
among dandelions
Another scratches in the brown earth
with one leg
bending her head for worms.
A dog barks in the distance.

Beyond the green picket fence,
there is a road
but not many cars travel it.

Elizabeth Brewster

Dreamtime

A child is in a house
and the house is on a street.

On other streets in other houses
other children sleep.

And parents creep from bedrooms
to kitchens bright below
to talk in muffled voices
of the children they love so.

A child in a quiet room drifts
towards the land of dreams.

A breeze outside the window
shifts the leaves in slant sunbeams.

And birds begin to whisper,
their day's last song is sung,
and evening, soft as feathers,
sighs that dreamtime has begun.

Deirdre Kessler

Total Recall

How do I remember you?
You liked brown bread,
And milk, and autumn leaves,
And white shirts, and a wide bed;
And any hill that soared,
And ships, and the grey sea,
And dogs, and old songs—
And you loved me.

How do I remember you?
You liked the spring,
And dawn, and daffodils,
And ebb tide, and a gull's wing;
And any kind of sweet,
And snow, and the blue sea,
And rain, and old books—
And you love me.

Eileen Cameron Henry

There's Only One You

There are catfish and flatfish and jellyfish, too,
There are all kinds of fish, but there's only one you.

And all of the wondrous fish in the sea,
Can't be as special as you are to me.

Tyne Brown

From *Apples and Butterflies*

I want to go where the moon is orange like the sun
and the stars go on forever
where marshmallows roast golden brown
and books come alive
late at night
over crackling campfires
I want to go where there are no alarm clocks
and no chores
only time
lots and lots of time

I just want to breathe
breathe air that tastes like apples:
      red
        ripe
          and ready for picking.

Shauntay Grant

Misty and Rain

Mom says the dogcatcher's not doing his job,
he ought to lock up those strays—
ruining the neighbourhood's roses—
she'll call the pound one of these days.
But dog's noses don't care about roses
and sometimes Mom likes to complain
Cause I'd rather be down at the end of town
jumping puddles with Misty and Rain.

Misty's a big bouncy Airedale
with mischief in her big misty eyes,
and Rain's a chubby young mongrel
with stubby legs small for his size.
He's covered in black and white speckles
like drops on a windowpane.
Yes, I'd rather be down at the end of town
jumping puddles with Misty and Rain.

It's fun to watch dogs perform in a show
saunter, parade, and do tricks;
it's fun to walk dogs that prance at your heel,
that jump hoops, shake, and fetch sticks.
But there are some dogs who won't sit up and beg
there are some dogs you just can't train—
And I'd rather be down at the end of town
jumping puddles with Misty and Rain.

Michael Pacey

Bear

How to care for a bear:

Bears tend to be shy at first,
so talk to him a bit,
find out what his name is.
Next, give his nose a squeeze,
rub his ears
and brush his hair.

Take him on a tour of the yard:
Show him the little corner of garden
you call your own.
Like a scarecrow
he'll watch over your seedlings
and growl away
the furry caterpillars.

At night on your white pillow
while the other animals
sleep beside you
your bear stands guard
at the head of your bed—
his small round eyes wide open.

Michael Pacey

The People Rainbow

When we open wide our eyes
when we look at each other
we see smiles and eyes and short,
                      long
                black, red, blonde, brown
                    and sometimes curly-curly hair

And we see faces like a rainbow all around
some are brown
and some are pink
and almost, almost white
(but not like snow)
some are like coffee
while some are golden, like wheat in a field

Black and brown and red and tan
all the colours of people
all the colours of the land

That's us
that's you,
and that's me too

We are colour.
We are the people rainbow.

Maxine Tynes

Warm Is a Circle

A circle is a bubble
floating
soapy in space

A circle is where I live
with spaces all around

An oval is an egg
A place to grow

Warm is a circle to curl up in.
A kitten is a place to warm my hands.
A warm kitten is a place to close my eyes and hear.

Wet is a place that I see,
where circles float
around me.

I put my head on a place to rest.
Rest is a place that is soft.

Rest is a place that is quiet:
a nest within the leaves.
A tree is quiet.
Quiet is a place we can see—
the birds and me.

When it is dark I rest.
Dark, where walls make patterns.

And when I wake I see
my window.
Light is a square in the wall.
A window is a place.
It is full of other places.

Hilary Thompson

Singing and Dancing

Sing me a morning song,
A wakey, stretchy, blinky song.
Sing me a morning song
To start my day.

Dance me a morning dance,
A barefoot, newfoot daybreak dance.
Dance me a morning dance
To start my day.

Sing me a happy song,
A smiling, la-la joyful song.
Sing me a happy song
Every day.

Dance me a happy dance,
A bouncy, snappy dappy dance.
Dance me a happy dance
Every day.

Sing me an angry song,
A howling, crying, sighing song.
Sing me an angry song
But not every day.

Dance me an angry dance,
A stamping, kicking, twisting dance.
Dance me an angry dance
But not every day.

Sing me a playtime song,
A laughing, shouting, sharing song.
Sing me a playtime song
Every day.

Dance me a playtime dance,
A hands together, whirling dance.
Dance me a playtime dance
Every day.

Sing me a bathtub song,
A swishing, splashing, gurling song.
Sing me a bathtub song
Every night.

Dance me a bathtub dance,
A scrubbing, rubbing, hugging dance.
Dance me a bathtub dance
Every night.

Sing me a sleepy song,
A bye-o-baby, hush hush song.
Sing me a sleepy song
Every night.

Dance me a sleepy dance,
A yawning, rocking, swaying dance.
Sing me a sleepy dance
Every night.

Anne Hunt

When I Was Small

When I was small
I used to help my father
Make axe handles.
Coming home from the woods with a bundle
Of *maskwi, snawey, aqmoq.*
My father would chip away,
Carving with a crooked knife,
Until a well-made handle appeared,
Ready to be sandpapered
By my brother.

When it was finished
We started another,
Sometimes working through the night
With me holding up a lighted shaving
To light their way
When our kerosene lamp ran dry.

Then in the morning
My mother would be happy
That there would be food today
When my father sold our work.

Rita Joe

Mactaquac Beach

I remember a spray of light.
Sky blue dark blue, and green across the lake
and red and white buoys.
I remember water droplets in a fanning arc
catching the sunlight like a cut glass chandelier.
I remember the hands catching me,
and the feel of a smile of the face of a tiny woman
with eyes the same colour as the sky.
I remember ducking in cool-warm water
down over my waist—dangerous depth—
I couldn't swim. I was two.
The water could never close on me
though it rushed up around my body
her hands always caught me
and up I went again,
laughing.

I only remember this:
one swing up, one anticipated plunge in the water.
I am hovering in memory at the top of the arc,
in a spray of light.

Kathryn Hunt

Maritime Baby

I'm a Maritime baby
I am, I am.
And I know what's a lobster
And I know what's a clam.

And I sail my boat
In a bathtub sea,
And I fish for fishes
for Nanny and me.

Shirley Downey

Rocking

Rocking in my rocking chair
(back and forth and back and forth)
slumped upon my mommy's lap
(back and forth and back and forth)
arms are wrapped around her neck
(back and forth and back and forth)
mommy softly rubs my back
and back and forth and
back and forth

hum so soft and sing so low
twinkling stars and blackbird pies
rock inside my mommy's love
warm and hugs, close my eyes

Gretchen Kelbaugh

Bedda-bye Maritime Rhyme

Dull-a-bee dusk-ee-ness
Dimm-ably darker-est
Baby-boo book-a-bye time

Pumble-pum puffins
Blueberry muffins
Drift-a-ling into the mist

Droop-sy your eyes
Butterfly byes
Marvelous maple-y kiss

Dandelion dotter-ing
Buttercup blotter-ing
Yellowy, mellowy yawn

Tenderly tuckering
Pinkish pout puckering
Spotily, tottle-y fawn

Grandiose greenery
Spellbinding scenery
Springing to sprout a spruce

Crooning, coniferous
Superbly, splendiferous
Magnificent moo-sical moose

Glistening gleamering
Drowsily dreamering
Silky city lights

Fireflies flickering
Peepers pip-pippering
Starry country nights

Deep down drawing in
Sawing a logging in
Limitless lengths of shore

Slumber-some sleepy head
Frondy furled fiddlehead
Tidal bore, rapidly roar

Blissfully blessfully
Rocking and restfully
Bedda-bye Maritime rhyme

Beth Weatherbee

Whispers

Mermaid

She seeks songs hidden among rocks
on Fundy shore, finds periwinkles

silent in tidal pools. Her cold fingers
pluck a rusty tin can from the sea,

fill it with winkles and water. Tail
slippery as eelgrass, eyes drowned

with knowing, at earth's edge
she conjures up needfire, settles her catch

in its heart. When driftwood transmutes
to purple smoke, water to silver fog,

rhythm of ocean will thrum in her throat,
salt fires dance on her tongue.

Janet Barkhouse

Birth of a Legend

Who came ashore last night in the dark?
Who came ashore in the lee of the light?
Where was it happened?
Who was to see?

Oh, they say there were women
And men in hip-boots
Shouting and scrambling
On the black slippery rocks.

But where was it happened?

Give me time will ye woman,
Let me say what they tell.

There were grey boats at anchor
and dories come in
then out dashed these figures
where the land drops right deep
but they slippered ashore
by MacDonald's, it's said.

But who was it saw this?
And what were their names?
Where did they go?

They hit for the woods
through the grass and the night
dragging their bones and letting
strange cries.

Oh, they say it was awful
the cries they let forth
like no gull on earth
like no human voice.

But who?

It was Fraser
and Willie wandering home,
Willie with fiddle and Fraser
quite drunk but playing
the pipes like you've never heard.
You'll never believe it
but they're swearing today
that something right awful
come out of the bay.

Douglas Lochhead

Nova Scotia Fish Hut

Rain, and blown sand, and southwest wind
Have rubbed these shingles crisp and paper-thin,
Come in:
Something has stripped these studding-posts and pinned
Time to the rafters. Where the woodworm ticked
Shick shick shick shick
Steady and secretive, his track is plain:
The fallen bark is dust; the beams are bare.

Bare as the bare stone of this open shore,
This building grey as stone. The filtered sun
Leaks cold and quiet through it. And the rain,
The wind, the whispering sand, return to finger
Its creaking wall, and creak its thuttering door.

Old, as the shore is. But they use the place.
Wait if you like: someone will come to find
A handline or a gutting-knife, or stow
A coiled net in the loft. Or just to smoke
And loaf; and swap tomorrow in slow talk;
And knock his pipe out on a killick-rock
Someone left lying sixty years ago.

Charles Bruce

Glasier's Men

Don't you hear them coming, tramping down the glen?
Husky, lusty giants, shades of Glasier's men?
Can't you hear them shouting, can't you hear them sing,
Marching on the Squattock in the early spring?

Leaders through the dappled dawn,
Wardens of the night,
Might all in girth and brawn,
Devils in a fight.

Don't you see the "Main John" striding in the lead?
Clear eyed, strong and fearless, kith of Bluenose breed;
First to bring a timber drive through the wild Grand Falls;
First to sight the Squattock Lakes where the lone moose calls.

Haunter of the silent ways,
Spirit of the glen
Dauntless as in olden days,
Glasier leads his men.

Glasier's men are driving, don't you hear their call?
Ghostly shadows gliding through the forests tall;
Inland stream and valley, sweeping plain and hill
Feel again the spirit of the old-time thrill.

Shogomoc is running wild,
Tobique's white with foam,
Once again the mighty drives
Are sluicing grandly home.

Glasier's men are calling—calling strong today—
From the forest-reaches where they led the way.
Stirring souls to action, lifting visions bright,
Thrilling hearts to daring, nerving arms to might.

Down the slopes of yesterday,
Through the throbbing years,
Comes the message ringing clear
Of Glasier's pioneers.

Hiram Alfred Cody

Note: John Glasier was the pioneer lumberman on the St. John River, and at one time employed over six hundred men. To distinguish him from his brothers, he was known as "Main John Glasier." He began his lumbering operations on the Shogamoc.

The Legend of Glooscap's Door

There is a doorway to Glooscap's domain
Where you throw dry punk and fish
For his fire and food.
But you must not enter
Though you may leave a gift on stone
Waiting to feel goodness.
This is the way the legend goes
So the Micmac elders say.

At Cape North on a mountain you whisper,
"My grandfather
I have just come to your door
I need your help."
Then you leave something you treasure
Taking three stones.
This is your luck.
This is the way the legend goes
So the Micmac elders say.

At Cape Dolphin near Big Bras d'Or
There is a hole through a cliff
It is Glooscap's door.
And on the outside a flat stone
It is his table.
The Indians on a hunt leave on table
Tobacco and eels.
This brings them luck, so the story goes
The legend lives on.

Rita Joe

The Boy Who Played The Guitar With His Feet

A little boy lived in an old packing box
In an alleyway off the street.
At night by the light
Of a street lamp bright,
He would play the guitar with his feet.

He would sing to himself as he sat on his shelf
Little tunes about being alone.
Sometimes he would weep
As he lay down to sleep
On the floor of his packing box home.

Some nights he would hide in the alley outside
Of a waterfront bar called *The Crow*,
He would hum the wrong words
To the songs he had heard;
He would strum the guitar with his toe.

Lance Woolaver

The Great Goblin's Song

Tonight we dance beneath the moon,
Above our land we go.
This is the last dance 'neath the moon
Until it melts all the snow.
So come you goblins, follow me
To dance beneath the moon,
And then we'll sleep the winter through,
'Til April, May, or June.

Mary Grannan

The Twilight Elf

    At evening when the shadows come
And it's almost time for bed
I wait beside the windowpane
And watch for Sleepy Ned.
    He's a funny little fellow
Who visits me each night,
Though I'm the only one who knows—
His step's so very light.
    He comes hopping from the shadows—
You might take him for a bird.
And I tap so he will see me
And he waves to show he's heard.
    He always does a little dance
Beside the tall elm tree,
And he is so very tiny
That I have to strain to see.
    At first his dance goes quickly—
His arms just whirl around,
His little feet are flashing
Upon the soft dark ground.
    But as the darkness thickens
His arms begin to slow,
His feet are scarcely moving
And he's stopped first thing I know.

    He fades away like magic
Every night just as I hear
My mother calling softly,
"It's time for bed now, dear!"
    But tomorrow when the shadows come
And it's almost time for bed,
I shall sit beside the windowpane
And watch for Sleepy Ned.

Desmond Pacey

A Bedtime Blessing

May Moonbeams mix with Fairy Dust,
A pinch of Love, a dash of Trust,
A rainbow and a star so bright,
A lullaby and Dawn's first light,
A dragon's scale, a mermaid's ring,
The soft caress of angel wing,
Combine in gentle darkness deep
To weave a dream as 'ere you sleep.

Jennifer Aikman-Smith

Sleepy Man

When the Sleepy Man comes with the dust on his eyes
    (Oh, weary, my Dearie, so weary!)
He shuts up the earth, and he opens the skies,
    (So hush-a-by, weary my Dearie!)

He smiles through the fingers, and shuts up the sun;
    (Oh, weary, my Dearie, so weary!)
The stars that he loves he lets out one by one,
    (So hush-a-by, weary my Dearie!)

He comes from the castles of Drowsy-boy Town
    (Oh, weary, my Dearie, so weary!)
At the touch of his hand the tired eyelids fall down,
    (So hush-a-by, weary my Dearie!)

He comes with a murmur of dream in his wings
    (Oh, weary, my Dearie, so weary!)
And whispers of mermaids and wonderful things,
    (So hush-a-by weary, my Dearie!)

Then the top is a burden, the bugle a bane
    (Oh, weary, my Dearie, so weary!)
When one would be faring down Dream-a-way Lane,
    (Oh, hush-a-by, weary my Dearie!)

When one would be wending in Lullaby Wherry,
    (Oh, weary, my Dearie, so weary!)
To Sleepy Man's Castle by Comforting Ferry,
    (So hush-a-by, weary my Dearie!)

Sir Charles G. D. Roberts

If I Were the Moon

If I were the moon,
I'd shine down my light
Right into your bedroom
To warm up the night.

If I were the ocean,
I'd sail you away
Then bring you back home
At the end of the day.

If I were a tree,
I'd let you climb high
You could talk to the squirrels
And tickle the sky.

If I were a flower,
I'd grow just for you
I'd dance in the wind
When you wanted me to.

If I were a snowflake,
I'd tickle your face
Then blow away laughing
In white open space.

If I were a rainbow,
I'd let you ride down
My kaleidoscope slide
All the way to the ground.

If I were a mountain,
You could reach for the sky
Then sing to the angels
While clouds drifted by.

If I were a song,
I'd hum you to sleep
I'd give you a dream
All your own just to keep.

But I am who I am,
And that's even better.
We'll all be together
Today
       And for ever…
and after.

Sheree Fitch

Afterword

Atlantic Canadian literature for children is a rich field to be harvested. Sewn liberally with whimsy, nonsense, nature, community, intellect, and soul, then cultivated over time and against multiple genres and literary traditions, it offers nourishment for the child in us all. As curator of the Eileen Wallace Children's Literature Collection at the University of New Brunswick, I spend my days surrounded by this rich harvest. Because of limited print runs, scattered availability, dwindling school library budgets, and the almost ephemeral nature of many publications for children and young adults, however, these materials are not always widely available in the classroom or for family or scholarly use. This is particularly the case for poetry, where often a poem's survival depends upon its appearance in an anthology.

A few years ago, Sheree Fitch and Anne Hunt approached me with a plan: to research and edit an historically and regionally comprehensive anthology of Atlantic Canadian poetry for children, the results of which you hold in your hands. Much of the research for this book took place in the Eileen Wallace Children's Literature Collection at the University of New Brunswick and with support provided from a Wallace Research Fellowship. Established by long-time New Brunswick librarian and educator Eileen Wallace, the collection has the largest academic holdings of children's literature in Atlantic Canada. It offers a snapshot of which books were popular with children in nineteenth- and twentieth-century New Brunswick and strives to collect comprehensively books for children and young adults by Atlantic Canadians as well as those which are set or published in the region. Without the professional dedication and financial generousity of Eileen Wallace over the years, many of the poems included in this anthology and the very history and tradition surrounding children's poetry in Canada's Atlantic provinces would be scattered, obscured, and difficult to track down.

Before their research even began, Sheree and Anne knew what the title of this volume would be: *Whispers of Mermaids and Wonderful Things*, from the Sir Charles G. D. Roberts poem "Sleepy Man." In choosing Roberts, Sheree and Anne revealed their deep understanding of how the categories of inclusion, through which we understand our personal and collective histories and upon which we peg our identities, are always fluid and contextual. A native of central New Brunswick (Douglas, Westcock, and Fredericton), Roberts's roots were firmly in Atlantic Canada, and yet, he was a cosmopolitan figure, living in New York, Paris, Munich, London, and Toronto. His imaginative landscapes, though, always grew from his New Brunswick origins, particularly the Tantramar Marsh area where he was raised. In addition to crossing great geographical distances in his life, Roberts crossed multiple genres in his work. He is most prominently remembered as "The Father of Canadian Poetry," yet he also has a substantial body of prose to his name and is widely credited with pioneering the modern animal story. The third terrain Roberts traversed is the wide age range of his readership, with poetry and stories that speak to adults as well as children. When Roberts "whispers of mermaids and wonderful things," you have a pretty good idea that he knows what he's talking about.

Similarly, this anthology anchors itself as a collection of Atlantic Canadian poetry for children; and yet the world these poems collectively creates refuses to draw its circle too tight around stereotypical, preconceived notions of region, childhood, or poetic form and style. This is a world of seascapes (Charles Bruce's "Nova Scotia Fish Hut") and cities (Mary Dalton's "St. John's Haiku"), and of imaginative landscapes (Fred Cogswell's "The Dragon Tree") alongside detailed descriptions of the natural world (Kenneth Leslie's "Three Tulips Stand and Talk to Me"). Nonsense (Kate Inglis's "Merman Ben") lies next to imagism (Elizabeth Brewster's "View from Window") and sometimes the two are combined, as in Lesley Choyce's "Three Ways to Remember Winter." Traditional rural work, as depicted in Hiram Alfred Cody's "Glasier's Men" and Rita Joe's "When I was Small," stands juxtaposed to contemporary urban occupations like that in Al Pittman's "Street Cleaning." The implied children of these poems cross many ages and circumstances, from the safety of the nursery (Sir Charles' G. D. Roberts's "Sleepy Man") to the perils of the street (Lance Woolaver's "The Boy Who Played The Guitar With His Feet"), and their perspectives are spoken of in the first person of discovery (Ed Yeomans's "At the Blue Moo Confectionary Store"), the second person of parental love (Jennifer Aikman-Smith's "A Bedtime Blessing"), and the third person of adult detachment (Kay Smith's "A Boy, A Tree, A Turtle Said"). Included in these pages are lyrics, limericks, riddles, haikus, bouncing rhymes, and nonsense verse. In the words of Jennifer McGrath, this book is simply "wordalicious."

    I remember the first day Sheree and Anne came in to the Wallace Collection to start work on this anthology. We dove almost immediately into the work of Grace Helen Mowat, whose "The Bay of Fundy" remains a perfect metaphor for their achievement with this book:

"I like the Bay of Fundy—
For when the tide is out,
So many wonders of the deep
Are scattered all about."

All these wonders were indeed scattered about, but now are pulled together between the covers of this book. I hope you have enjoyed the low-tide walk its pages have provided and that you will return time and again to explore its pools.

Dr. Sue Fisher
Curator, Eileen Wallace Children's Literature Collection,
University of New Brunswick
December 2016

Poet Biographies

Milton Acorn: 1923–1986
Born in Charlottetown, Prince Edward Island, Milton Acorn was known as "The People's Poet." He received the Canadian Poet's Award in 1970 and the Governor General's Award in 1976.

Jennifer Aikman-Smith is an author and illustrator living in Moncton, New Brunswick. She has illustrated three children's books. *A Lullaby for New Brunswick*, published in 2012, was her first work for very young readers.

Vella Pearl Aiton: 1893–1988
Special grandmother, friend, and neighbour; garden gloves and floppy hats; daffodils and sunshine; gingersnaps and Christmas dinners; Canasta and Scrabble; a camp on the lake; hugs and smiles; sharing and caring; avid reader; hobby poet who expressed her thoughts on the happenings of the day, including wartime.

Janet Barkhouse lives on the South Shore of Nova Scotia. She has had an interesting career as an actor, an educator, and a fiction writer. She has also written plays for children. She began writing poetry in 2006.

Joyce Barkhouse: 1913–2012
Born in Woodville, Nova Scotia, Joyce Barkhouse began writing in

1932 but was not published until 1974. In 1989 she wrote *Pit Pony*, which was later produced as a CBC Television film and Gemini Award–winning television series. She received the Order of Nova Scotia in 2007 and the order of Canada in 2008 for her contributions to children's literature.

Brian Bartlett grew up in New Brunswick but has lived in Halifax since 1990. His many books of poetry include *The Watchmaker's Table*, *The Afterlife of Trees*, and *Granite Erratics*, and he has also published a book of prose, *Ringing Here & There: A Nature Calendar*. "Falcon on a Dark Day" is a poem he published in his late teens and recently revised for this anthology.

Jane Baskwill lives in rural Nova Scotia. Her writing career was launched early in her life when, according to her website, her parents allowed her to write on the walls of her room. She is a former teacher and principal and has written picture books, a novel, and a collection of poetry for children. She has also authored a range of professional materials for teachers. She has a deep appreciation for nature and is an advocate for social justice. Six times she has received the Education Quality Award from the Nova Scotia Teachers' Union.

William Bauer: 1932–2010
Bill Bauer was born in Portland, Maine, and came to Fredericton to teach at the University of New Brunswick in 1965. He taught for thirty years in his adopted home and was a respected professor, mentor, and poet with a unique sense of humour.

Elizabeth Brewster: 1922–2012

Elizabeth Brewster grew up in Chipman, New Brunswick. She began writing poetry when she was nine years old and published her first collection of poetry, *East Coast*, in 1951. She attended the University of New Brunswick, Radcliffe College, University of Toronto, and Indiana University. She worked as a librarian and English professor and was involved in forming *The Fiddlehead*, Canada's longest-running literary magazine.

Tyne Brown's work has appeared in numerous children's magazines and literary journals. Her first book, *Driftwood Dragons and Other Seaside Poems,* was shortlisted for the 2013–14 Hackmatack Children's Choice Book Award. She is the recipient of the Joyce Barkhouse Writing for Children Award and a Nova Scotia Talent Trust Award.

Charles Bruce: 1906–1971

Charles Bruce was a newspaperman and poet who grew up on the north shore of Chedabucto Bay. He won the Governor General's Award for Poetry for his collection *The Mulgrave Road*.

Bliss Carman: 1861–1929

Bliss Carman was born in Fredericton. He attended the Collegiate School there and, along with his cousin Charles G. D. Roberts, was introduced to poetry through his teacher George Parkin. His first book of poems, *Low Tide on Grand Pré: a Book of Lyrics*, was published in 1893. His poetry celebrates the Maritime landscape.

Lesley Choyce is a novelist and poet. He teaches at Dalhousie University, runs Pottersfield Press, and is a member of SunPoets, a spoken-word rock band. He also hosted *Off the Page*, a national TV show. He lives in Lawrencetown Beach, Nova Scotia, where he is a year-round surfer.

George Elliott Clarke, Canada's Parliamentary Poet Laureate and the fourth Poet Laureate of Toronto, was born in Windsor, Nova Scotia. He currently teaches at the University of Toronto. His work focuses on "Africadians," a word he created for the Black population of Nova Scotia and New Brunswick.

Hiram Alfred Cody: 1872–1948
Hiram Alfred Cody came from the small village of Codys, New Brunswick. His mother loved poetry and recited many poems to her children. Cody learned them and liked to recite them while working in the fields. The family created their own newspaper, *The Jolly Band*; Cody wrote the local news column. He later attended King's College in Windsor, Nova Scotia, where he was the editor of its newspaper. He served as an Anglican priest for many years and published numerous short stories and novels.

Fred Cogswell: 1917–2004
Fred Cogswell was born on a farm in East Centreville, New Brunswick. He attended a one-room schoolhouse where he excelled in reading, writing, and mathematics. Afterwards he attended normal school, taught, briefly, and in 1940 enlisted in the army. After the war he enrolled in the University of New Brunswick, where he studied until 1949. He received his PhD from the University of Edinburgh,

and returned to teach at UNB in 1952, becoming editor of *The Fiddlehead* literary magazine. His work as a poet and as a translator of Acadian poetry has been widely published and he has mentored many of Atlantic Canada's young poets.

Theodore Colson spent his entire teaching career at the University of New Brunswick, where he also served on the editorial board of *The Fiddlehead*. He was a member of The Ice House Gang, a group of poets who met to share and workshop their poems each week in The Icehouse on the campus. He won the Alfred G. Bailey Award for Writing in 1985. He is an avid salmon fisher.

Helen Creighton: 1899–1989
Helen Creighton was a Canadian folklorist who collected songs and stories of Nova Scotia and New Brunswick. She was born in Dartmouth, Nova Scotia, and attended Halifax Ladies' College and McGill University. She also served as Dean of Women at the University of King's College. She was the Canadian Distinguished Folklorist of 1981, a Fellow of the American Folklore Society, Honorary Life President of the Canadian Author's Association, and a recipient of the Order of Canada.

Mary Dalton is the author of five books of poetry, among them *Merrybegot*, *Red Ledger*, and *Hooking: A Book of Centos*, released in 2013 by Véhicule Press. A prose collection, *Edge: Essays, Reviews, Interviews*, was published by Palimpsest Press in the fall of 2015. A letterpress chapbook, *Waste Ground*, is forthcoming from Running the Goat Books in 2017.

Lynn Davies was born in Moncton, New Brunswick. Her family owned a bookstore and her mother read and recited poems to her and her sister. She attended the University of King's College, receiving the Silver Medal in English. She worked as a freelance journalist for a time and then, after taking time to raise a family, she published her first poetry collection, *The Bridge That Carries the Road*, in 1999. She enjoys sharing her passions of writing and hiking with children.

Tom Dawe is best known for his poetry but is also a painter and has written several books for children. He was born in Long Pond, Conception Bay, Newfoundland, and was educated there and at Memorial University, where he taught English until his retirement. He was a founding editor of *TickleAce*, Newfoundland's literary magazine, and co-founded the publishing company Breakwater Books.

Shirley Downey is dedicated to early childhood literacy. She is the founder of Born to Read, a program for newborns in the province of New Brunswick. The program inspired her to write and publish books for young children. She grew up in St. Stephen, New Brunswick.

Juliana Horatia Ewing: 1841–1885
Juliana Horatia Ewing was born in Ecclesfield, Sheffield, England. Her mother, Margaret Gatty, was a children's author and Juliana followed in her footsteps, authoring several novels for children. In 1867 she married Major Alexander Ewing and they moved to Fredericton, New Brunswick, where her husband was posted. She adopted Fredericton as her home, writing many letters to her family back in England about the beauty of the landscape and warmth of the people.

Reshard Gool: 1931–1989

Reshard Gool was a poet and novelist who lived in Charlottetown, Prince Edward Island, and taught at the University of Prince Edward Island.

Mary Grannan: 1900–1975

Mary Grannan was born in Fredericton, New Brunswick. She wrote stories for her CBC Radio and Television shows for children, *Just Mary* and *Maggie Muggins*. These stories were later published as a series of books.

Shauntay Grant is a writer and storyteller from Halifax, Nova Scotia. Her honours include a Best Atlantic-Published Book Prize from the Atlantic Book Awards, a Poet of Honour Prize from Spoken Word Canada, and a Joseph S. Stauffer Prize in Writing and Publishing from the Canada Council for the Arts. She teaches creative writing at Dalhousie University.

Zach Hapeman is a writer and illustrator working in Fredericton, New Brunswick. He has a Master's degree in English from Acadia University and tours throughout New Brunswick schools sharing his unusual humour and storytelling with students of all ages. He has published two children's resource books with Standard Publishing and his children's poetry has appeared in *The Caterpillar* magazine. His first book of poems and drawings, *A Crack in the Door*, was published independently in 2016.

Christopher Heide is from Prince Edward Island. His collection, *Poems of a Very Simple Man*, was published in 1978. He has also written several plays and directed theatre companies in Nova Scotia including Mulgrave Road, Liverpool International Theatre Festival, Chester Playhouse, and Mermaid Youth Theatre.

Eileen Cameron Henry: 1908–2000
Eileen Cameron Henry had her early education in New Glasgow, Nova Scotia, and attended Dalhousie University. After her marriage she moved to Antigonish where she served on the town council, always working for the poor and disadvantaged. She received the Order of Canada, the Queen Elizabeth Medal, and was named Woman of the Year in Nova Scotia. She had a column in *The Antigonish Casket*, "Around Town and Country," and published two books of poetry.

Kathryn Hunt grew up in New Brunswick and started writing poetry in grade school. She won second prize for children's literature in the New Brunswick Writers' Association annual competition when she was fourteen; that book was later produced as a radio play by CBC Radio's *Atlantic Airwaves*. Many, many poems later, she now lives in Ottawa, Ontario, where among other things she is a member of the Ottawa StoryTellers, edits a community newspaper, hosts a literary radio show, writes about cycling, and, in summer, spends as much of the weekend as possible rock climbing.

Kate Inglis lives on the South Shore of Nova Scotia. She has written and published the middle-grade books *The Dread Crew: Pirates of the Backwoods* and a sequel, *Flight of the Griffins*. Her third book, *If I Were a Zombie*, is a collection of monster poetry for children.

Rita Joe: 1932–2007
Rita Joe was known as the Mi'kmaq Poet Laureate. She was born in Wycocomagh on Cape Breton Island, Nova Scotia, and was sent to the Shubenacadie Residential School. She wrote about this experience in *Songs of Rita Joe*, published in 1989. She published six other collections of poetry, received the Order of Canada in 1992, and was one of the few non-politicians appointed to the Queen's Privy Council.

Heddy Johannesen has always wanted to be a writer. Her writing has been published in a variety of journals. She lives in Halifax, Nova Scotia, where she is owned by two pets: a kitty named Penny and a guinea pig named Magic. She grows a herb garden, sews, and devours books in her spare time.

Virtue Keen: 1858–1929
Virtue Keen was born in Cape Cove, Newfoundland. Legend has it she wrote *Lukey's Boat* about a local fisherman and performed it at a concert held at a local church hall.

Gretchen Kelbaugh, mother of three, grandmom of four, teacher of science, poetry, and filmmaking, social activist, humourist, and hockey player—a very slow hockey player, who falls quickly and for no reason.

Deirdre Kessler is a poet, novelist, teacher, and broadcaster. She was the host of CBC's *The Story Show*. She teaches children's literature at the University of Prince Edward Island.

Carole Glasser Langille is the author of four books of poetry, two collections of short stories, and two children's books. She has been nominated for the Governor General's Award in poetry, the Atlantic Poetry Prize, and the Alistair MacLeod Award for Short Fiction, and her children's book *Where The Wind Sleeps* was selected for the Our Choice Award by the Canadian Children's Book Centre. In 2015–16 she was Artist/Writer in Residence at the Dalhousie Medical School. She currently teaches Creative Writing at Dalhousie University.

Joanne LeBlanc-Haley grew up in a family where the oral tradition of telling stories, reciting poetry, and singing songs was practiced. As a parent, grandparent, and educator, she continues to have ample opportunity to engage in the oral tradition. Joanne lives in Fredericton, New Brunswick, where she is currently in a doctoral program at the University of New Brunswick.

Kenneth Leslie: 1892–1974
Kenneth Leslie was born in Pictou, Nova Scotia. He began writing poetry at an early age. He also loved to sing and play the piano and violin. He has published several collections of poetry and a collection of songs, *Songs of Nova Scotia*. He won the 1938 Governor General's Award for his collection *By Stubborn Stars*.

Douglas Lochhead: 1922–2011
Douglas Lochhead spent his childhood summers in Duck Cove, just outside Saint John, New Brunswick, and, after a career as a librarian and teacher that included founding the library at Massey College in Toronto, returned to Sackville, New Brunswick, where he became

director of Canadian Studies at Mount Allison University. He later became writer in residence. Many of his poems reflect the landscape of the marshes.

Hugh MacDonald received the L. M. Montgomery Children's Literature Award in 1990 and the Award for Distinguished Contribution to the Literary Arts on Prince Edward Island in 2004. In 2010 he was appointed Prince Edward Island's Poet Laureate. He lives in Montague, Prince Edward Island.

Kim McAdam has lived in Grand Bay, New Brunswick, most of his life where he was influenced by some wonderful teachers who sparked his interest in literature and writing. During his thirty-eight years of employment at Moosehead Breweries, he continued to write for the joy it brought him and others. He was a finalist in the 2013 Writers Federation of New Brunswick competition in the children's literature category. His three-year-old granddaughter, Alyssa, is his "biggest fan."

Jennifer McGrath writes novels, picture books, and poetry for children. She studied at St. Francis Xavier University and then at the University of Victoria, where she received a Master's degree in Children's Literature. She lives just outside of Moncton, New Brunswick.

Hallie Rose Mazurkiewicz was born in upstate New York in 1990 and moved to Fredericton, New Brunswick, as a child. It was there that she learned the language of Atlantic Canadian sunsets and how to pen poetry in the snow. Hallie currently resides in New York City where she is a writer, educator, and self-proclaimed student of life.

L. M. Montgomery: 1874–1942

Lucy Maud (L. M.) Montgomery is best known for her novels, of which she published over twenty, *Anne of Green Gables* being the most popular. However, she also published over five hundred short stories and a collection of poems. Her work has received international attention. She was born on Prince Edward Island which is the setting for many of her novels. Her first published work was a poem, "On Cape LeForce." It appeared in the Charlottetown *Daily Patriot* in 1891.

Grace Helen Mowat: 1875–1964

Grace Helen Mowat was born in Beech Hill near St. Andrews, New Brunswick. After completing her early education at the Charlotte County Grammar School, she studied art in England and then at Cooper Union Institute in New York City. She taught briefly in Halifax before moving back to St. Andrews where she founded Charlotte County Cottage Craft, encouraging women to produce crafts of original design which were then sold for profit in larger urban centres. She published several local histories and a poetry collection, *Funny Fables of Fundy and other Poems*.

Alden Nowlan: 1933–1983

Alden Nowlan was awarded the Guggenheim Fellowship and the Governor General's Award for Poetry. He was born in Nova Scotia and left school at age ten. He worked in the village sawmill and hitchhiked eighteen miles to the regional library to get books. At nineteen he took a job at *The Observer*, a newspaper in Hartland, New Brunswick. It was then that he began writing poetry. In 1966 he became writer-in-residence at the University of New Brunswick. While there he also collaborated with Walter Learning to write several plays.

Ellen Bryan Obed was raised on a small farm in Maine, but spent many years in Labrador. There she married into the Inuit culture and raised three children. She also taught, studied Labrador's flora, wrote poetry and children's books. Her favorite genre? Poetry. The favourites of her books? *Borrowed Black, A Labrador Fantasy* and *Twelve Kinds of Ice,* a story in twelve vignettes of the skating of her childhood.

Desmond Pacey: 1917–1975
Desmond Pacey was born in New Zealand, spent his early years in England, and moved to Canada in 1931. He studied at the University of Toronto and later Trinity College, Cambridge, where he developed an interest in Canadian Literature. He was professor and head of the department of English at the University of New Brunswick. His book *Creative Writing in Canada: A Short History of English-Canadian Literature* (1952) brought him national recognition. As the father of seven children, he was inspired to write two collections of verse for children and two collections of short stories.

Michael Pacey is the son of Desmond Pacey. As a student at Fredericton High School, he and his friend Brian Bartlett started a creative writing club. The two attended the University of New Brunswick where they joined The Ice House Gang, a group of established writers. Michael travelled to University of British Columbia for graduate studies and published his first children's book, *The Birds of Christmas*. He now lives and works in Fredericton.

Ferne Peake: 1916–1968

Ferne Peake lived in Murray Harbour, Prince Edward Island. She wrote hundreds of poems, particularly about the beauty of the island. Her daughter, Pamela Logan, recently edited and published a collection of her work, *Memory Isle: Poems by Ferne Peake*, to fulfill the dying wish of her mother, who had been working on the collection at the time of her death.

Al Pittman: 1940–2001

Al Pittman was a Newfoundland poet and playwright and co-founder of Breakwater Books. His work often focussed on outport life. His collection of children's poems, *Down by Jim Long's Stage: Rhymes for Children and Young Fish* (1976) was republished in a celebratory twenty-fifth-anniversary edition. He was writer in residence at Sir Wilfred Grenfell College in Corner Brook, and in 1999 was inducted into the Arts Council Hall of Honour.

Edwin John (E. J.) Pratt: 1882–1964

Edwin John Pratt was born in Western Bay, Newfoundland. He graduated from St. John's Newfoundland Methodist College. He received a BA and a Bachelor of Divinity from Victoria College, University of Toronto, and later, in 1917, his PhD. He taught at Victoria College until his retirement in 1953. The library at the college is named after him. He is a three-time winner of the Governor General's prize.

Sir Charles G. D. Roberts: 1860–1943

Sir Charles G. D. Roberts was born in Douglas, New Brunswick. He attended Collegiate School in Fredericton and the University of New Brunswick. His first poetry collection, *Orion and Other Poems*, was published in 1880. He is often referred to as "The Father of Canadian poetry." He, Bliss Carman, Archibald Lampman, and Duncan Campbell Scott are know as the "Confederation Poets."

Norene Smiley is a writer and visual artist who, no matter what she is creating, is enamoured with "story" and its structure, and how you go about sharing it. She has written picture books, flash fiction, poetry, and screenplays. She loves digital media and has created three short films. Her watercolour and acrylic paintings are figurative, concerned with gesture and narrative.

Kay Smith: 1911–2004
Born in Saint John, New Brunswick, Kay Smith's first poem was published when she was only fourteen years old. She attended Mount Allison Ladies' College and after graduation founded a nursery school in Saint John. She was active in the Saint John Theatre Guild and taught at Saint John Vocational School and directed the annual Shakespeare play. Her poetry appeared in several poetry magazines, including *The Fiddlehead*. Summers spent on Grand Manan inspired much of her work.

Hilary Thompson: 1943–2009
Hilary Thompson was a writer, artist, and English professor at Acadia University. She pioneered and championed children's literature as a field of scholarly study in English departments, and shepherded and mentored many students—including Sheree Fitch. She studied

at the Universities of Aberdeen in Scotland and then Alberta, where she received a PhD in 1972. Wife to Ray and mother of three, this collection of poetry is dedicated to an amazing woman who touched many lives. May her work, her deep appreciation of poetry, and her generosity of spirit long be remembered.

Maxine Tynes: 1949–2011
Maxine Tynes was born in Dartmouth, Nova Scotia, a descendent of Black Loyalists. Her first book of poetry, *Borrowed Beauty*, published in 1987, won the Milton Acorn People's Poetry Award. She was the first African Canadian to sit on the Dalhousie University Board of Governors.

Doug Underhill was born in Newcastle, New Brunswick, and has lived and taught in Miramichi for his entire career. He received the New Brunswick Outstanding Teacher Award in 2000. He has published three poetry collections, three children's books, two folklore books, a sports book, and a Miramichi dictionary. He has also written for the Moncton *Times and Transcript* and the *Miramichi Leader*.

Steve Vernon grew up in a hockey town and can skate with the grace of a dying moose with frostbitten hooves and his slapshot has all the power of a flaccid ramen noodle. His books include *The Lunenburg Werewolf, Haunted Harbours, Wicked Woods, Halifax Haunts*, the children's picture book *Maritime Monsters*, and the YA novel *Sinking Deeper—or my Questionable (Possibly Heroic) Decision to Invent a Sea Monster*.

Ken Ward left home by train at the age of eight to begin his exploration of the world and he refused to grow older. In time he began to write poetry for children and draw pictures that captured the delight and absurdity that engineers his curious mind. Ken has made magic in a wide range of activities, including making superb butter tarts, teaching nonsense to the serious minded, and stepping in to save arts organizations when no one else will.

Beth Weatherbee is the author of *Bedda-Bye Maritime Rhyme*, published by the UNB Early Childhood Education Centre for the Born to Read NB initiative. She is also a co-author of *Follow the Goose Butt, Camelia Airheart*, with Odette Barr and Colleen Landry, who will be releasing the second in the series, *Take Off to Tantramar,* in 2017. Baie Verte, New Brunswick, is where she makes her home with nine cats, three rabbits, two dogs and a husband in a ~~pear tree~~ round house.

Budge Wilson, a graduate of Dalhousie University, was born and raised in Halifax. She has received numerous awards, including the Order of Canada and the Order of Nova Scotia. Her prolific writing career began in 1984 with the publication of *The Best/Worst Christmas Present Ever*. A recent publication, *Before Green Gables*, a prequel to *Anne of Green Gables*, has been published in eleven countries and translated into seven languages.

Kathleen Winter was born in England and raised in Newfoundland. She is best known for her short stories and novels, among which was *Annabel*, shortlisted for the Giller Prize and a Canada Reads selection. However, her writing career began as a scriptwriter for *Sesame Street*.

Lance Woolaver was born in Digby, Nova Scotia, and currently lives in Halifax. He has written plays and film scripts as well as poetry.

Jennifer Wyatt grew up in the country outside of Fredericton, hearing and playing all kinds of music. She read everything she could get her hands on, hiding under the covers with a flashlight in order to keep reading after "lights out." She moved to Halifax, Nova Scotia, to be by the sea, and after her husband built her a Celtic harp she began writing songs.

Ed Yeomans: 1927–2009

Ed Yeomans published a poetry collection, *The Green Dragon and other Poems*, in 1976. He was born in Saint John, New Brunswick, and educated at the Universities of Mount Allison and Toronto. He taught school in rural New Brunswick before moving to the west coast, where he taught English at the University of Bristish Columbia.

Permissions

Poems not listed below were either previously unpublished and provided courtesy of the authors or are in the public domain.

Excerpt from *Apples and Butterflies* by Shauntay Grant is taken from the children's book, with illustrations by Tamara Thiebaux Heikalo, Halifax: Nimbus Publishing, 2012.

"The Beagle and the Beluga and the Eagle's Fine Times" by Sheree Fitch was originally published in *If You Could Wear My Sneakers!*, illustrated by Darcia Labrosse, originally published by Firefly Books in association with UNICEF, 1997, 1998, and republished by Nimbus Publishing, 2017.

"Bedda-Bye Maritime Rhyme" by Beth Weatherbee was originally published with illustrations by Chrissie Park-MacNeil, Fredericton: University of New Brunswick, 2015.

"Birth of a Legend" and "A Poet Swings at Christmas" by Douglas Lochhead were originally published in *The Full Furnace: Collected Poems*, McGraw-Hill Ryerson, 1975.

"Dreamtime" by Deirdre Kessler was originally published in *Dreamtime*, illustrated by Christina Patterson, PEI: Acorn Press, 2011.

"Glasier's Men" by Hiram Alfred Cody was published in *Fifty-four narrative poems*, edited by O. J. Stevenson, Toronto, 1933.

"A Gommil From Bumble Bee Bight" was originally published by Harry Cuff Publications Ltd.: St. Johns, Newfoundland, 1982.

"Halifax Boys" was originally published anonymously in *Uncle Jim's Canadian Nursery Rhymes*, edited by David Boyle and illustrated by C. W. Jefferys. Toronto: Musson Book Company, 1908.

Excerpts from *Lasso the Wind* by George Elliott Clarke were originally published in the collection *Lasso the Wind: Aurélia's Verses and Other Poems* with illustrations by Susan Tooke, Halifax: Nimbus Publishing, 2013.

"May" by Helen Creighton was originally published in *With a Heigh-Heigh-Ho: Stories and Verse for Children*, illustrated by Bill Johnson, Nimbus Publishing, 1986.

"Mrs. Kitchen's Cats" by Ken Ward was originally published in *Mrs. Kitchen's Cats*, Toronto: Annick Press, 1990.

"November" by Milton Acorn was originally published in the collection *In Love and Anger*, privately issued in Montreal, 1956. It was recently republished in *Milton Acorn: The People's Poet*, Blackpoint, NS: Roseway Publishing, 2015.

Excerpt from "The Boy Who Played Guitar The With His Feet" by Lance Woolaver was originally published in *Change of Tide*, with drawings by Anna Gamble, Nimbus Publishing, 1982.

"The People Rainbow" and "What Can I Do for the World Today?" by Maxine Tynes were originally published in *Save the World for Me*, Lawrencetown, NS: Pottersfield Press, 1991.

"Port Elgin Evening" by Doug Underhill was originally published in *River Poems*, Nepean, ON: Borealis Press, 2007.

"Singing and Dancing" by Anne Hunt was originally published in the series *Books for Children and Families*, Early Childhood Centre, University of New Brunswick, 2002.

"There's Only One You" by Tyne Brown was originally published in *Driftwood Dragons and Other Seaside Poems*, Nimbus Publishing, 2012.

"Through Dark Trees I See the River" was originally published in *The Beauty of It* copyright 1980 by Theodore Colson. Reprinted by permission of Goose Lane Editions.

"Uncle Tom" and "Young Clem Clam" by Al Pittman were originally published in *Down by Jim Long's Stage: Rhymes for Children and Young Fish*, Newfoundland: Breakwater Books, 1976. Reprinted with permission of Breakwater Books.

"Tantrum Poem III" and "Unsnarling String X" were originally published in *Unsnarling String* copyright 1983 by William Bauer. Reprinted by permission of Goose Lane Editions.

"The Legend of Glooscap's Door," "Untitled," and "When I Was Small" by Rita Joe republished with permission of Breton Books on behalf of the Estate of Rita Joe. "Untitled" was previously published in *Song of Rita Joe: Autobiography of a Mi'kmaw Poet*, 2011; "When I Was Small" was previously published in *The Blind Man's Eyes: New and Selected Poetry*, 2015.

"View from Window," first published in *In Search of Eros*, Toronto: Clarke, Irwin, 1974, and "March Afternoon" by Elizabeth Brewster are reproduced with permission of the University of Saskatchewan.

"Warm is a Circle" was originally published in *Warm is a Circle*, Lancelot Press, 1979.

Excerpt from *Where the Wind Sleeps* by Carol Glasser Langille was originally published with illustrations by Tom Ward, Black Point, NS: Roseway, 1996.

Index

A

Acorn, Milton
  "November" 44
Aikman-Smith, Jennifer
  "A Bedtime Blessing" 140
Aiton, Vella Pearl
  "The Saint John in Winter" 45

B

Barkhouse, Janet
  "Mermaid" 128
Barkhouse, Joyce
  "Annapolis Valley" 38
Bartlett, Brian
  "Falcon on a Dark Day" 67
Baskwill, Jane
  "In Grandma's Attic" 104
  "Pass the Poems Please" 11
Bauer, William
  "Tantrum Poems III" 95
  "Unsnarling String X" 26
Brewster, Elizabeth
  "March Afternoon" 35
  "View from Window" 108
Brown, Tyne
  "There's Only One You" 111
Bruce, Charles
  "Nova Scotia Fish Hut" 131

C

Carman, Bliss
  "An April Morning" 36
  "The Flute of Spring" 37

Choyce, Lesley
  "Three Ways to Remember Winter" 49
  "URENTIT" 19
Clarke, George Elliott
  From *Lasso the Wind*
    "New leaves!" 39
    "The ocean's a lot" 55
Cody, Hiram Alfred
  "Glasier's Men" 132–133
Cogswell, Fred
  "Full Circle" 53
  "The Dragon Tree" 52
Colson, Theodore
  "Through Dark Trees I See the River" 63
Creighton, Helen
  "May" 40

D

Dalton, Mary
  "St. John's Haiku" 60
Davies, Lynn
  "Here, then Gone" 25
  "My Incredible Leanamabobber" 12
  "Typhoon Alice" 31
Dawe, Tom
  "A Gommil From Bumble Bee Bight" 84
Downey, Shirley
  "Maritime Baby" 122
  "The Balloon Man" 83

E

Ewing, Juliana Horatia
  "Canada Home" 106

F

Fitch, Sheree
  "If I Were the Moon" 142
  "On the Road to Everywhere" v
  "The Beagle and the Beluga and the Eagle's Fine Times" 14–15

G

Gool, Reshard
"The Bottom" 16
Grannan, Mary
"The Great Goblin's Song" 137
Grant, Shauntay
From *Apples and Butterflies* 112

H

Hapeman, Zach
"Unfinished" 27
Heide, Christopher
"Black Cat" 69
Henry, Eileen Cameron
"Total Recall" 110
Hunt, Anne
"Singing and Dancing" 118–119
Hunt, Kathryn
"Mactaquac Beach" 121

I

Inglis, Kate
"Merman Ben" 87–88

J

Joe, Rita
"The Legend of Glooscap's Door" 134–135
"Untitled" 107
"When I Was Small" 120
Johannesen, Heddy
"The Saw Bug's Toil" 71

K

Keen, Virtue
"Lukey's Boat" 98–99
Kelbaugh, Gretchen
"Little Millipede" 20
"Rocking" 123
Kessler, Deirdre
"Dreamtime" 109

L

Langille, Carole Glasser
From *Where the Wind Sleeps* 57–59
LeBlanc-Haley, Joanne
"Concert in the Forest" 74–76
Leslie, Kenneth
"The Whale and the Frog" 96–97
"Three Tulips Stand and Talk to Me" 70
Lochhead, Douglas
"A poet swings at Christmas" 17–18
"Birth of a Legend" 129–130

M

MacDonald, Hugh
"Dead Man's Pond"; "Hot Foot" 82
"Wet Feet"; "Toes" 81
Mazurkiewicz, Hallie Rose
"Once Upon a Pine Tree" 101
McAdam, Kim
"But I Don't Like Peas" 93–94
"Reuben Rat" 85–86
McGrath, Jennifer
"The Joob-Joob Jungle" 13
"WORDALICIOUS" 10
Mowat, Grace Helen
"Spinning Wheel Song" 43
"The Bay of Fundy" 56

N

Nowlan, Alden
"In the Garden" 80

O

Obed, Ellen Bryan
"North Dance" 33

Index ~ 169

"Rhubarb" 72
"Sky Carver" 34

P

Pacey, Desmond
  "The Twilight Elf" 138–139
Pacey, Michael
  "Bear" 114
  "Misty and Rain" 113
Peake, Ferne
  "Yesterday's Storm" 30
Pittman, Al
  "Street Cleaning" 103
  "Uncle Tom" 23
  "Young Clem Clam" 24
Pratt, E. J.
  "A Feline Silhouette" 64
  "The Shark" 65

R

Roberts, Sir Charles G. D.
  "A Wake-Up Song" 41
  "Sleepy Man" 141
  "The Piper and the Chiming Peas" 102

S

Smiley, Norene
  "The Winter Yard" 46–47
Smith, Kay
  "A Boy, A Tree, A Turtle Said" 61

T

Thompson, Hilary
  "Warm Is a Circle" 116–117
Tynes, Maxine
  "The People Rainbow" 115
  "What Can I Do for the World Today?" 77

U

Underhill, Doug
  "Port Elgin Evening" 32
Unknown
  "Halifax Boys" 100

V

Vernon, Steve
  "Frozen Freedom" 48

W

Ward, Ken
  "Mrs. Kitchen's Cats" 21
  "The Platypus" 22
Weatherbee, Beth
  "Bedda-bye Maritime Rhyme" 124–125
Wilson, Budge
  "Eating" 90–91
Winter, Kathleen
  "Her eyes on the Horizon" 54
  "On Etiquette Day" 92
Woolaver, Lance
  "The Boy Who Played The Guitar With His Feet" 136
Wyatt, Jennifer
  "Just Summer" 42

Y

Yeomans, Ed
  "At the Blue Moo Confectionary Store" 89